A MAGIC DOOR

AND

A LOST KINGDOM OF

PEACE

A Collection of Tales

by

H.D. Hunter

Illustrations by Donahue Johnson

Published by H.D. Hunter

ISBN: 978-0-692-63326-7

Illustrations, including cover, by Donahue Johnson
Cover design by Patience Woodill
Edited by Clare Wood, Self-Publishing Services LLC (www.Self-Publishing-Service.com)
Formatted by Self-Publishing Services LLC (self.publishing.services@gmail.com)

Obsessed by a fairy tale, we spend our lives searching for a magic door and a lost kingdom of peace.

Eugene O'Neill

For Charli

Table of Contents

Acknowledgements

The author wishes to acknowledge the sources of quotations used in this book.

Epigraph for *A Magic Door and A Lost Kingdom of Peace*: O'Neill, Eugene. *Long Day's Journey into Night*. New Haven: Yale University Press, 1956. Print.

Epigraph for "Best Friends":

Schinz, Marina, and Susan Littlefield. *Visions of Paradise: Themes and Variations on the Garden*. New York: Stewart, Tabori & Chang, 1985. Print.

Epigraph for "Real Monsters":

Dickinson, Emily, Mabel Loomis Todd, and Thomas Wentworth Higginson. *Poems by Emily Dickinson*. Boston: Roberts Brothers, 1890. Print.

The Southern District

I dream about the Southern District every night, but we must begin with the day, and so we will.

I wake up at eight a.m. Normally, I lay in bed until about 8:05. Then, I try to get out of bed without waking my roommate. I always check the weather on my laptop and then dress accordingly. I leave the room and pull the door quietly shut and then make my way down the hall to the bathroom. At 8:11, I begin brushing my teeth. I brush for five minutes or so. After I'm finished, I return to my room, where I grab my bag and coat. Once I have everything I need, I try to leave without disturbing my roommate. Normally, I fail.

I lose track of time for the rest of the day. I've missed class several times just from walking around campus for too long. Father says it's because I don't own a watch. He says all real men should own a watch. I think all real men should be themselves. Besides, he is not my father anyway. He has been around since I was a baby though, so Mother insists I call him Father. Either way, I lose track of time because the days mean nothing. Each day is a twenty-four hour obstacle impeding my path to the next recess from school. On school holidays, I get to travel home and be comfortable in my natural habitat.

After I leave my room, I take the long walk to the dining hall so that I can eat breakfast. I can't remember the last time the sun was shining. It's normally cold and windy. The scenery makes me feel like I'm walking around in an old black-and-white movie.

People scurry around in all directions with their heads down, probably to keep the wind off of their faces. Or maybe it's so they don't have to look at each other. When I get to the dining hall, I pick up whatever they are serving that day because most of the time it all tastes the same. I sometimes sit at the table behind the stone column next to the kitchen. It's easier to hide there. I always sit alone. It used to bother me, but not any more. After I'm done eating, I attend my first and second period classes, and then I go to lunch. I always pass Tiffany on my way to lunch.

I say, "Hi, Tiffany," and wave.

She says nothing.

Father often says I speak too softly. Maybe she never hears me.

Lunch is normally tasty. A stampede of people rushes both ways in front of me as I eat. I see some people I know, and some of them speak to me. Sometimes I see Helen at lunch, the pretty girl from the first floor of my building. One day, she smiled at me. I raised my head from my plate and swallowed a bite of chicken sandwich.

I said, "Hi, Helen."

She laughed and walked away. I checked the sides of my mouth for fragments of food but didn't find any. Maybe she thought of something funny.

I return to my room after class is finished, and my roommate is still asleep. He is very lucky. I do homework for the rest of the day and sometimes I eat dinner, but sometimes I don't. On some nights, I go to bed early so that I can get to the Southern District earlier. I lay in bed looking at the ceiling, trying to drown out the monstrous snores drifting from across the room. Sometimes I believe my roommate is not a student but a homeless man, living free of room and board at expense of the college. I muffle my laughter with my pillow as I think about this. The last thing in my mind before I arrive in the Southern District is my roommate, the slyest homeless man alive. I laugh to myself until I fall asleep.

I am there.

"Welcome to the Southern District," the lady usher says.

I walk in confidently and start to meander. The Southern District is the largest building you can imagine. It is like a shopping mall with infinite floors and endless stores that stock everything you need. The wide walkways branch into stores that sell clothes, food, medicine, cars, books, music, and even confidence. That's right, boxes of confidence. I don't remember, but I'm sure I bought my confidence in the Southern District some time or other because it only works when I'm there. The walls are vibrant blues, yellows, and reds. Music blares over the speaker system in the Southern District. They play all the best songs, and the playlist is infinite. Everyone is in costume. Your costume reflects your personality. I am always dressed as a lion. Helen is dressed in all black. Maybe she is a witch.

One time I was dressed as a peacock, but every other time I am a lion. I walk through the halls of the mall for what seems like hours. I see all of the people I go to school with. Tiffany and I walk arm in arm, followed by Helen and all the rest of the people I often see but do not know. Our steps echo in unison on the golden floors. Sometimes I wear a top hat over the mane of my lion suit. After we all dance, sing, and walk for a while, a bell starts to ring. Everyone is sad because they know this means the Southern District will end soon. People slowly start to fade away. The colors of the walls blend together and swirl around the room. The bell rings louder and louder in my ears. A strong breeze carries the giant color swirl away, and everything is gray scale as the bell becomes unbearable. My head pounds until I feel like screaming. In fact, I try to scream, but no sound comes out.

I am awake.

Yesterday in class we learned about utopias and dystopias. We talked about George Orwell and Thomas More.

I raised my hand and asked, "So, the Southern District is a utopia?"

Professor I-Know-Everything said, "I know nothing of a *Southern District.*"

What's in a name, right?

He kept talking, and I could hear the boy two seats down from me snickering. I am not mad. I just wish he would be my friend and not snicker at me.

I called Father after class because Mother says I should call him regularly to show I care. Sometimes I don't know if I care, but when I know for sure, I call. I told him about the Southern District and how badly I wish that it was real.

He said, "You can't live in a dream world, Son."

I tried to explain how much better the Southern District is than the real world, how sometimes I take sleeping pills so I can fall asleep at seven or eight so that I can be in the Southern District longer. I told him about my lion suit, the boxes of confidence, and how sometimes, if I look hard enough, I can find my roommate sleeping in the home furnishings store in the Southern District. He only said what he always says.

"Just try to make some friends. We all miss you. I've got to get back to work now. Good-bye."

Father doesn't listen or understand very well. I wish Mother could hear Father talk like this. Maybe she wouldn't make me call him, if she only knew.

Father says you can't live in a dream world. The thing is, you can't die in one either.

Last night, when I fell asleep, all I saw was black. I woke up, and I didn't know what to do. I got out of bed and took more pills, but I never left. I stayed in my bed all night, trapped and crying in the empty darkness.

So this morning, I skipped class. I didn't worry about waking up my roommate when I got out of the bed. I didn't check the weather; I looked you up on the Internet instead. I called, and you agreed that I could stop by. I came in and lay down on this comfortable couch, and you told me to talk. I told you my story. You know about Tiffany, utopias, and the Southern District. Can you help me? I mean, can you make it real? Don't diagnose me; I know what's wrong. I'm alone; I'm depressed. I've lost control. I don't want medicine. Please don't give me medicine. I don't want to have to come see you again. I want to see colors. Blues, yellows, reds. I want the lady usher to know my name. I want to hear music that you can't help but dance to and walk on golden floors. I want them to wave back when I wave at them first. I took a cab here because you told me you could help. I want to walk arm in arm with pretty girls and wear a lion suit. I'm tired of eating alone. Have you ever been to the Southern District? I want to sleep. If I sleep forever, I'll never have to leave. Is that how I make it real? I want Father to understand the things I say. Can you help me?

Hatari Forest

The marble slid out of Charles Peregrine's hand and hit the dusty, wooden floor with a hollow thud. The sound jolted Charles out of his half-sleep. He picked up the marble and resumed twirling it between his thumb and forefinger. The candle was almost burnt out, but Charles didn't mind. Sometimes he watched in the dark. He was peering out of a small window that looked out over the backyard of his family's cottage. The small cottage was home to him, his younger brother Nathaniel, his mother, and his father, for whom he was waiting by the window. He awaited his father this way most nights, worried for him. He never really could sleep well before Mr. Peregrine came home for the night.

The wind whistled and cut across the land, adding a deadly chill to the cool night air. It had become cold unusually fast that year, and by mid-October, most folks had bundled up as if in the heart of winter. As Charles drifted to sleep again, a softly glowing orb appeared in the woodlands behind the house. It got larger and larger until it exited the woods, bobbing slightly up and down as it approached the cottage. Charles awakened and noticed the orb. He immediately rushed from his room, out the front door, and around the back of the house. Isra Peregrine was maybe thirty yards away, trudging slowly through the tall grass outside of the cottage fence. He wore his long brown coat and wide brimmed hat. Even though the hat was tattered—Isra had owned it since he was a teenager—he wore it all of the time, even in harsh weather. It was his favorite hat. His father had given it to him on their first hunting trip together. As he stepped into the yard, he was met by Charles hugging his leg tenderly. Isra patted the boy on the head and motioned to him so that he would follow his father inside.

Once they were inside, Charles helped Isra take off his boots and coat. He looked up at his father while he removed his socks. Isra's eyes were bloodshot and glassy. Under his coat, his shirt hung loosely on his shoulders. Nathaniel would normally help too, but Isra had come home later than usual tonight. Their mother would be upset, but not once she saw what Isra had brought home.

"Did you get anything good, Papa?" Charles asked.

Isra took his hand out of his pocket and unfolded his palm to reveal a handful of shining, golden coins. Charles looked up in amazement, giddy with excitement. Isra smiled and let out a bellowing laugh.

"Mama is going to be so happy!"

"Yes, yes she will. But now, it's time for bed."

Charles lay in bed, excited about how the night had gone. He had noticed his mother crying earlier that day, as it had been a long while since the family could afford to go to the market. Now that his papa had brought money, she would be happy again. He was glad that his papa had gone into the forest. Every time he went into the forest, he came back with money. Even when Mama cried and screamed at his papa for going there, it was okay in the end because he always came back with money. Charles thought that the traders on the other side of the forest must be very rich. His father was a great hunter, but for any hunter to sell *all* the game he ever caught was unheard of. Charles was also happy because Isra had been nice to him after returning home. *There was no hitting tonight and no yelling, either. He was happy to see me tonight.* Yes, it had been a good night. The last sound Charles heard before drifting off to sleep was the violent, guttural coughing of his father.

***

"Boys...I'm very sick."

Nathaniel and Charles sat outside the cottage on a tree stump. It was a brisk day, but the sun was high in the sky without a cloud for company. The boys had been outside playing a game that involved chasing each other around in a never-ending transfer of the duty for one to capture the other. Their mother stood in the doorway on the porch of the cottage, watching from afar with her arms crossed. She was much too far away to hear the conversation.

"What's wrong, Papa?"

"Oh, just a disease that old folks get...but it eventually gets them." Isra coughed twice and swallowed hard. His throat felt like sand. It was hard for him to breathe the sharp outdoor air.

"I have to take one of you into the forest, so you can learn how to hunt."

"But we already know how to hunt, Papa," said Nathaniel.

It was true. The boys had accompanied their father on hunting trips many times. They had learned to use the bow and the rifle, as well as all the tools used for cleaning and preparing the meat after the animal was killed. Even though they were young boys, they had a knack for hunting and took to it quite naturally.

"Yes, you're right, Nate. But now, you must learn what I do at night."

"You mean when you bring the money?" asked Charles.

"Mmhm." Isra nodded. "One day, I'll be gone. One of you is going to need to know how to make money for the family when times are hard, just like I do. It's different at night. It's dangerous. But as you saw last night, Charles...I always come back with money."

"Yes, Papa."

The boys looked down at their shoes and fidgeted uncomfortably. Death was no stranger to their hamlet. Pneumonia had swept through the village last winter and claimed the lives of many of their schoolmates' parents. A girl two years above Nathaniel in school, Mindy Landon, had drowned earlier that summer at the lake. Mr. Piper, the owner of the book shop, had disappeared maybe six months earlier and never returned. His daughter Vega had lived on her own for a while before a neighboring family took her in. She ran away from their house frequently, but they tried to bring her back. She said she was looking for him. She wanted to find her father.

Even with their familiarity with death and despair around the village, the boys didn't take hearing their father talk about his impending demise any easier. He coughed throatily as he talked to them about manhood and responsibility, sometimes doubling over, clutching his gut, and gasping for air. After a couple of fits, Nathaniel ran into the house to get a jug of water, hoping the soothing drink might ease Isra's ailments. Isra continued talking through the fits, adamant about helping his sons understand the gravity of the situation.

"I will need to take Charles, for he is older and more prepared."

"Aww, Papa…" Nathaniel sulked. He had always secretly felt that he was his father's favorite. He was right. Jealousy burned his ears, and Charles continued to look at his shoes. He kept his head down so neither his father nor his brother would see the smirk emerging on his face.

"Charles will teach you when I am gone, Son. But I must prepare him first. He is the oldest. It is the right way."

Their mother began to sob and moved from the doorway back into the cottage. Maybe she could hear from where she was standing, after all.

***

Charles lay awake all night, the covers pulled up over his head, feet rubbing against each other rapidly in excitement. He would have a chance to make Papa so proud by learning to hunt with him in the night. The last time he had gone with Papa in the day, he had done well, but he missed the last deer of the hunt with his bow, and Isra had been disappointed. It was to Charles as if all of the rabbits and other small game he had caught that day were worthless. Once Papa was upset with him, nothing mattered anymore. Tomorrow was the last day of the weekend before school, and in nearly twenty-four hours, he would be walking deep into the woods with Papa, probably carrying that soft, glowing orb he had watched creep out of the trees so many other nights before. The excitement was too much to bear. The birds had begun the first light's chorus before Charles's case of the heavy eyelids flared up again.

The boys awoke early for their daily chores. Nathaniel shook Charles, who had just barely fallen asleep, awake so they could get dressed. Each enjoyed a crust of toast and milk before heading outside. Even though it was early, their mother had already gone to the market, so she would be back with better food later. Charles cleaned the chicken coop while Nathaniel fed the birds. After, both boys took turns chopping kindling. After the boys finished chopping, they headed out back to the shed. It was almost midday, and the sun was high in the sky. It was a warm day, but still brisk when the boys went to the shed for more chores. They took to tightening the bows, counting the arrows, and cleaning and loading the rifles; they were preparing for the hunt that night. Charles had finished tightening his favorite bow and gathering his arrows in the quiver next to it when he turned around to face the entrance of the shed and was met with the barrel of a rifle.

"What are you doing, Nate?" Charles asked, muffled but indignant.

Nate said nothing but kept the barrel pointed right between Charles's eyes and inched it a little closer to touching his skin. The gun was loaded. Charles had watched Nate put the shells in.

"Remember how Papa told us he was shooting them bears out there in the woods?...What you think about maybe I shoot you like how he was shooting them bears? I'm a better hunter than you, anyhow. I don't know why Papa is taking you," Nate said bitterly.

"Whatever, Nate," Charles said, grabbing hold of the barrel and trying to move it out of his face. Nathaniel thrust it toward him, and to avoid being hit in the face with the gun, Charles ducked. When he ducked, he lost his footing and fell on the floor of the shed. Nathaniel pounced on top of him and started hitting him furiously. Nate continued to beat Charles forcefully. Even though he was younger, he was maturing fast, and once he had overpowered Charles, it didn't take much effort to keep him subdued. The sound of the shed door flying open and slamming against its outside wall startled both boys, and Nate's fists finally stopped flying. They turned and saw their father standing in the entrance, his chest heaving up and down. He walked over and roughly pushed Nate off of Charles. He yanked Charles up by the arm and dragged him out of the shed, slamming the door shut behind him, leaving Nate inside.

Isra dragged Charles all the way through the tall grass to the edge of the woods in their backyard.

"Why are you fighting with your brother?!" he screamed.

Charles froze in fear. No matter how familiar the situation, he was afraid of his father and could never quite muster up enough courage for a good showing, which only made his father angrier.

"What? Stop murmuring! He's your brother. You can't hurt him. You're supposed to take care of him! What are you going to do when I'm gone?! Is this how you're going to act?!"

Isra, with a hold on Charles's shoulders, shook him savagely as he yelled, spit launching from his mouth onto Charles's face and neck. His face grew red from exertion, and during the parts of the shaking where Charles was pulled closest to his father's face, he could see tiny beads of sweat sliding down his father's brow to the bridge of his nose. Some of the beads ended up dripping from his nose on to Charles, joining the saliva that had earlier taken refuge there. Isra, winded from such abrupt, intense activity, tossed Charles down to the ground, exasperated. He wheezed out one phrase before turning and walking back toward the house.

"Nightfall. Right back here. Be ready. Your life changes tonight."

When his father was far enough away, Charles began to cry. He was in pain from the shaking and the earlier beating that Nathaniel had given him, but he was used to beatings. He cried because as his father walked toward the cabin, he had wished that Isra was already dead instead of sick and dying. He had never had a thought like that before. In his mind, he had officially become an evil person. And even though Charles immediately felt repentant after the thought, he was inconsolable. Through teary eyes, he saw that Nate had exited the shed and was standing ten yards away, watching him cry. He pretended not to see him and rolled over, uttering his muffled cries into a mound of leaves red and brown, freshly dead and doomed. He peeked back to where Nate had been standing maybe ten minutes later, but he was gone. Charles sat at the edge of the woods for the next few hours, feeling empty. As the sun started its westward descent, he gathered himself and walked back toward the cabin. His mama would be angry that he didn't wash off before laying down, but he felt exhausted. He sneaked into the house quietly, hoping not to disturb anyone, as everyone normally relaxed in separate rooms before bed. He got to the room he and Nate shared and noticed that Nate was not there—probably out playing somewhere. He crawled under his bed—the only place his father never looked when he was ready to shake him from his sleep and beat him—and drifted away to sleep faster than he could notice.

When Charles opened his eyes, it was dark inside the cabin. He scrambled from underneath the bed and looked out the window. He had missed dusk. He felt his heart start to slam inside his chest, and the back of his neck started perspiring. He pulled on an extra pair of socks, his boots, a jacket, and a warm hat. He dashed out of the house straight to the shed where the guns were. He scolded himself in his mind for being late and unprepared. He knew Isra would be upset. As he slung his bow and arrows over his shoulder, the shed door opened and Isra entered.

"You're late, come on."

"Sorry, Papa...I....I'm just going to grab the gu-"

"You won't need it."

Charles put the rifle and the shells down, but he kept his bow and arrows with him as he followed Isra out of the shed. They walked back toward the edge of the woods. Once they got to the spot where Isra had shaken Charles half to death earlier, Isra spoke calmly.

"This is Hatari Forest. It stretches for miles and miles both west and south of here. Most folks in this town have never seen the other side. It's very dangerous at night. 'Lotta nocturnal critters in here. I see you brought your bow. You might need it, never know. You ready?"

Charles nodded meekly.

"Every time I go into this forest, I bring home lots of money for you and Nate and your mother, remember? I'm going to show you how it's done. Stay close to me. We have a long way to walk."

Charles had heard the stories about Hatari Forest. Folktales that parents and teachers would tell kids, especially around bonfires or Halloween time. It was a forest of evil and danger. There were all types of creatures and people lurking within the woods in the stories. Man-eating dogs, trickster sorcerers, poison plants, and vines that would strangle you—each story had an explorer dying in a gruesome way, or entering the forest and never escaping. Charles had never paid them much mind as he knew they were only tales and not real. But he had never known that Hatari

Forest was a real place, and he certainly had no clue that he lived right on its edge. He was enveloped by the chill of the air as he entered the forest. He wondered if anything he had heard about the forest was real. *No, that's silly*, he thought. But his mind wandered as he walked, exploring all of the possibilities. He struggled to keep up with Isra's long strides, but he stayed as close to his father's hip as he could. As Isra crunched through the underbrush, Charles remembered one story about his distant neighbor who had gone into Hatari Forest and never returned.

His name was Aristotle Piper. He owned the only bookshop in the hamlet in which Charles's family lived. His daughter, Vega, was in class with Charles, but he didn't know her that well. Aristotle was a mouse of a man, beady eyes with a long nose on the tip of which sat circular, silver-rimmed glasses. His hair was white and thinning, raked back over his jellybean-shaped head. He was a foreigner who had moved to the town one summer years earlier, with just his daughter, no wife. By the time the summer had ended, Aristotle had bought an out-of-business boutique in the downtown square. He and Vega worked all fall to clean and patch the place up, and before the townspeople knew it, he was having truckloads of books delivered to the building. He and Vega had built all of the shelves themselves. He was very close with his daughter, Aristotle was. And Vega loved him with double the force in remembrance of her dear mother and in observance of all her father did to raise her alone. Once the books arrived, Aristotle hired a few kids from the town to work as librarians and stockers.

He carried most of the schoolbooks kids in the town needed, in addition to other leisure reading for the adults. Even though you had to pay, most folks in the town grew to much prefer Piper's Pages to the local library, which was dirty, outdated, and understocked. He saw much success for several years. Folks presumed that Aristotle had become a pretty wealthy man, and there were rumors that he was looking to open bookshops in the surrounding towns.

And then one day, he disappeared.

He couldn't have been gone for long when the townspeople noticed he was missing. Piper's Pages was always the first shop open downtown, its chimney smoking out over the capitol building as the sun rose in the late fall and winter. When the police, who had been alerted to his absence by some other shop owners, got to his cabin, they found it in normal condition. They were led to the back of the house by faint whimpers and sniffles. They found Vega in the back room wrapped in a blanket, crying. They couldn't get a word out of her; she just cried louder and louder, so they took her to the station, gave her some hot chocolate, and wondered where in the world Aristotle might be. After a while, they heard Vega speak up from the corner of the room.

"I knew he wasn't coming back."

Vega explained the events of the night before, when Aristotle had come home late from the bookshop. He said he had met with some of the town council after work about ways to build revenue. He was planning on investing partly in a mill project that would help boost the town's economy of textiles, which was its staple. To do this he would need more capital than his current bookstore, although lucrative, could provide. The discussion had arisen during the council meeting about the market on the other side of Hatari Forest; how the town directly on the other side was growing, and merchants there were ready for commerce. Some of the councilpeople said that they knew potential investors in the town who might be willing to defray some of the investment costs for another bookshop in exchange for some of the profits from the shop. Aristotle was excited at the possibility of franchising Piper's Pages and wanted to explore the new shop opportunity immediately. He decided that he would pass through the forest that night into the town. It was a long journey, so he planned to get into the town by sunup. He would meet with the investors, rest for the day, and begin to travel back at dusk. He would lose a day in the shop, but he gave Vega the key and instructed her to open the bookshop on her way to school, because he had asked one of the Henley boys who was no longer in school to run the shop for the day.

Vega, in fear and desperation, clung to his coat as he tried to leave the cottage.

"Daddy, there are...there are monsters in that forest! They all come at night, and you won't be able to make it through. I don't want you to go." She had, of course, heard the stories. Aristotle himself had told some of them to her during their arduous days building shelves. He knelt down and leaned into Vega so that the tip of his nose rested on the tip of hers.

"I love you, little one," he said. "Do not fear for me. There is nothing in those woods that can pull me so hard that I won't come back to you."

With that, he kissed her nose and strode out of the cottage toward Hatari Forest. Vega said she immediately went to her room and started to cry, hence the state in which police found her in the morning. She said she knew he was never coming back when he left. She just felt it. She was right.

Vega had started living with the Henleys, but would run home to her cottage and get in through the window every single night. One night, they never went for her. So teenage Vega Piper lived all on her own in the cottage she used to share with her father, about six miles from Piper's Pages. The shop had stopped accepting book shipments, growing cold, dark, and cobweb-ridden for the first time since it had opened. Vega came to school some days, and some days she didn't. It seemed as if everyone in the town was so unsure of how to deal with her that they let her deal with herself. Spring bloomed and flowed into summer. Most people forgot about Vega. She quite possibly became a character in the newest Hatari Forest folklore, *The Bookkeeper and His Daughter*; the story of a man who vanished without a trace, and his daughter, who kept such a low profile that she practically did the same.

Isra and Charles were fairly deep in the forest now. It was as dark as pitch: the closeness of Charles to his father the only thing keeping them from losing each other. All of a sudden, Isra's great strides stopped. He kneeled down and lent his ear to the wind. Charles did the same, and in the distance, he heard what sounded like cackling.

"Papa," he whispered, but Isra only covered his mouth with his hand. The cackling grew louder as it moved closer to where the father and son kneeled. Isra pulled Charles behind some bushes and motioned him to look out to where they had just been standing. It was then that Charles saw the source of the cackling. Five large creatures entered the clearing from different angles, making the dreadful noise all the way there. They were large and humpbacked, with wispy, spotted fur and eyes that glowed a pale yellow through the fog of the night. The creatures reminded Charles of the pictures of hyenas he had seen in his schoolbooks. Only these hyenas looked much more vicious.

"Shark dogs," Isra whispered as low as he could.

He didn't have to whisper; they had terrible hearing. Their sight, while not the best, was better suited for night than day. Shark dogs relied on their noses for hunting. Their sense of smell was elite, especially when it came to blood. The animals were dastardly. Although they were primarily carnivorous scavengers, they preferred their carrion still alive, badly injured even. They liked the torture. They liked doing the killing but didn't want to have to work so hard for it. They were named such for their abnormally abundant rows of sharp, flesh-tearing teeth that, like sharks', regenerated throughout their lives as old ones fell out. They always traveled in packs of three or more, and it was sure to be a long night for any creature that encountered them during one of their hunts.

They crept through the night, several of them cackling to each other every few steps. One of them strolled just a few steps away from the brush that the Peregrines were hiding in. It stopped and sniffed the air. Charles was so scared his knees began to shake, making rustling sounds on the leaves beneath. His father pulled him close and restricted his movement. The shark dogs started cackling loudly and circling each other. One came very near the bushes they were in and stuck his nose in the brush. Charles whimpered, and the shark dog looked up, right into his eyes. The dog's eyes were a pale yellow by the light of the moon. It seemed to almost smile, baring the rows and rows of sharp, stained teeth. It began a low cackle, which picked up in volume and frequency with each passing second. The other shark dogs cackled in unison and began to make their way over toward the brush. The first dog started pawing devilishly at the brush. Isra slowly reached into his belt strap and removed a hatchet. The dog would be fully through the brush in just a moment. The rest of them now joined him in pawing at the bushes, teeth showing, saliva dripping, their bedeviled cackle echoing through the night.

All of a sudden, a thundering roar drowned out all of the cackles. After a brief moment of silence, another roar boomed through the night air. The shark dogs scrambled and turned to face the largest creature Charles had ever seen. Arms outstretched, eyes glowing yellow-green in the dark, and quickly charging the bush in which Charles and Isra hid, was a creature most had only ever seen in a storybook...or their nightmares.

"Bull-bear," whispered Isra, entranced.

The bear stood no less than ten feet tall. Its legs were broad and mighty, which made a running, climbing, or swimming escape very unlikely. It was covered in jet-black fur aside from a triangle-shaped patch of neon fur on its chest that matched its eyes, and some said these creatures had ended up in Hatari as the result of a genetic modification experiment gone wrong. But most didn't believe in conspiracies, the same way they didn't believe in Hatari Forest. Its arms were long and muscular, ending in backpack-sized paws with claws sharp enough to filet any prey, beast or man. Atop the bear's huge shoulders stood its thick neck and head, the latter of which was adorned with two ivory-white horns, each four feet long with sharpened ends, hence, the derivation of the creature's name. In nightmares and fantasies, the bull-bear was a force to be reckoned with.

All of the shark dogs, much to Charles's surprise, charged the bull-bear as it bounded toward the bush. Each one began jumping up and sinking its teeth into the massive bear, although it seemed unfazed by most of their attacks. It swatted shark dogs left and right as it trudged on toward the bush, but the shark dogs were persistent. Those that had been smacked down quickly gathered themselves and retaliated. One of the smaller ones climbed up onto the shoulders of the bull-bear while two of his counterparts attacked each leg. The bull-bear spun around, shaking several of the dogs off, and as he continued to spin, one shark dog that had been previously shaken charged and leapt toward the bear's face. The timing was such that with the slightest thrust of the head, the Bull-bear impaled the leaping shark dog straight through, catching him on his horn and then quickly detaching the shocked, still-writhing body. The shark dog hit the ground and let out a yelp amidst a furious convulsion. The other shark dogs paused momentarily, but only long enough to process what had happened and then continued to cackle. The cackle had transformed from a jovial laughing sound to a high-pitched, agonized screaming. The small shark dog once again jumped up on the shoulders of the bull-bear as his brothers attacked and began pawing madly at the bull-bear's eyes. Another ferocious roar escaped the bear before it dropped to its knees. All of the shark dogs crowded around, their cacophony of cackling more sinister than ever. Charles felt himself being pulled backward, farther and farther away from the animals. Isra was holding him. Isra was running. They were escaping.

They stopped in a small clearing once Isra could no longer run and needed to catch his breath. He kneeled over a stump, huffing and heaving and coughing, hands on his knees. Charles wanted to comfort him, but he was too scared to move. His legs rattled together as he tried to stand up straight, but the numbness of his limbs made him feel woozy. After a few moments, his father's breathing stabilized, and Charles wondered who would be the first to speak.

"They're coming closer to town," Isra muttered.

"Huh?"

"The shark dogs. We weren't supposed to see them for at least another five, six miles into the woods. Same with the bull-bear. I've never seen one that close to the outskirts of Hatari."

This statement scared Charles. He clutched the strap to his arrow quiver.

"What does it mean, Papa? Will the creatures take over the town? I didn't think those sorts of things were real. I'm scared."

"There's no need to be scared. You know the truth now. Everything that you've heard about Hatari is real. Very real. Left uncontrolled, the creatures inside could very quickly and easily infringe upon human life. They could kill all of us in a day if they wanted to."

Charles felt like he had a rock in his throat. "...wanted to?"

"Yes, Son. These are no ordinary creatures in Hatari. These monsters are not bound by evolutionary instinct. Some are imbued with evil spirits, some have the choice of conscience, free will. They know what it means to kill, and they like it."

"Papa," Charles started nervously. "Why are we here?"

"I'm the guardian of Hatari Forest, Son," Isra said after a moment. "Our town and the town on the other side both pay me to hunt and kill the most dangerous creatures in this forest so that we might see continued peace and safety in our lands. I enter the forest on a hunting night, locate my prey, kill it, and take it to the town on the other side, where I'm paid once I present the hide of the creature. When I return to our town in the wee hours of the morning, a city official is waiting at the edge forest to see if I return alive. When I do, he pays me a second time."

It was all too much for Charles. He had always known his father was a great hunter. He had learned many of his own skills from traveling the forest in the daytime with his dad. But he had never gone at night. There were so many questions. Why was this a secret? Did the hellish animals only appear at night? Was Isra trying to train him to be the next guardian?

"Papa, it's so dangerous; why didn't we bring our best weapons?"

"Weapons are not the keys to survival, but rather instruments to assist in achieving that end. We must not rely on them but our instincts instead. You must learn the forest. Its twists and turns. Its creatures, its traps. You must come within an inch of your demise and live with that experience seared into your soul. Weapons won't do you any good until after then. You'll be the first snack on the menu whatever night you go into the forest."

"How are we going to escape, Papa? I feel like you brought me here to die." Charles began to cry.

Isra looked off into the distance. The white in his beard shimmered by the light of the moon as the wind blew a slight chill through the night. "Most men would rather die than see the things I've seen. Pick up your bow. We have far to go."

And with that, they trekked on.

They walked for many miles through the woods, up and down hills, around swamps and lakes. So many thoughts invaded Charles's brain as his father explained that Charles was to become the new guardian of Hatari. He felt so young and unprepared. For the first time in his life, he wished his father had chosen Nathaniel over him. Isra taught Charles about the forest as they traveled, but it was too much to remember. There were poisonous plants and insects, and streams that were hundreds of feet deeper than they appeared; there had even been talk of a hermit or two who liked taking advantage of little children who got lost in the forest. Charles had either read about these things or heard about them during bonfire stories, but his mind was paralyzed at the thought they could actually be real. When Isra wasn't talking, they walked along in silence, Charles clutching his bow at every rustling or whistling sound he heard. When Isra noticed Charles tense up, he would knock him to the ground and tell him to "let the fear go." Charles tried his best to stay aware and alert, yet calm.

As they walked through one section of the forest, the trees hanging overhead began to display a soft, orange glow. Charles looked up and all around. Tiny orange balls hung from the trees and vibrated with a low, humming sound.

"These neon orbs are berries—,"

That was all Charles heard.

The humming sound grew louder and louder and eventually took on the form of a hymn. The melodic tune made Charles want to close his eyes and breathe in the music. He couldn't close his eyes, however, because the soft, orange glow of the berries was so marvelous. He wanted to get closer. As he approached the low-hanging orbs on the trees, the hymn grew even louder. The berries looked so juicy and delicious, and he found that when he put his face close to the individual orbs, they would begin to rotate. Slowly at first, like the Earth on its axis, but after a couple of a seconds the berries would level-up to a dizzying spin that made Charles want to grab at them to keep them still. He grabbed at a few of them clumped together and was delighted to find that they came off the branch quite easily. The berries were ripe, and a couple of them burst between his palm and fingers, their sticky juice crawling across his hand. Charles licked his palm, unknowingly punching his ticket for a trip to a euphoric state.

He had barely tasted the sweet nectar pooled on his palm when he tossed a berry into his mouth and began to chew it slowly. His legs no longer felt woozy. The entire forest lit up in a blaze of oranges, greens, yellows, and pinks, and the humming hymn was more soothing than ever. Charles used his tongue to push the half-chewed berry from one side of his mouth to the other. It tasted so good; he didn't want to chew it completely. Charles's whole body felt very warm. He hadn't been this relaxed in weeks. Nothing seemed so bad anymore. He could handle the forest. The creatures weren't as scary as they had initially seemed. Isra wasn't so mean after all.

Isra threw his fist as hard as he could and caught Charles squarely in the jaw. Charles was unconscious before his face hit the damp, cool soil of the forest floor.

***

When Charles came to, a strange man was sitting on the forest floor, just feet away from him. Charles was immediately nervous. It was dark, and he wasn't quite sure where he was. He tried to lift his head and felt his jaw throbbing violently. His head was wrapped tightly from the bottom of his chin up around the top of his head, and he could not move it very well. He caught the man's attention when he tried to move, and when they locked eyes, Charles became terrified. He started to scramble away, but the man steadied him, grabbing his shoulders and whispering, "Charles…Charles..." Charles was surprised that the man knew his name. He calmed down and let the man speak. His hoarse voice was the only sound in the dark woods at that time. Between coughs, the man started to speak.

"Do you know who you are?"

"...I'm Charles."

"Do you know *where* you are?"

Charles hesitated. He had faintly remembered coming into a forest, but now that the man had asked him, he wasn't quite sure.

"I'm...I'm not sure. I know I'm in a forest."

"Yes, okay, but what forest? Do you know why you're here? Do you know who I am?"

Charles thought hard. Where was he? Why had he come here? He couldn't remember anything.

"Let's try this," the man said. "Do you remember coming here?"

"Yes. I left at night. I came with a man."

"What man?"

"My father."

"Where is he now?"

"You are my father."

"Yes, Charles. I am your father. What else do you remember?"

"We came here at night. We walked through the forest...and I fell asleep."

"No, Charles. Think harder. Why did we come here?"

Charles thought hard. Faint memories started to pull together in his mind. He had come to the forest at night. He thought he had come to hunt, even though he only had a bow and arrow. He and his father wanted to travel in the forest and hunt, but they got cornered by some cats...or maybe it was large dogs. Then there was a bull in there somewhere too. Then he must have tripped and fallen on his face because he remembered walking, and the next thing he knew he was asleep. And now his jaw was swollen and sore, and he couldn't remember anything. He explained all of this to the man he was pretty sure was his father, hoping for corroboration.

"Hm…" Isra pondered. "You're close. I'm worried. I can't give you too much, or it will ruin your memory. You have to remember on your own. If I tell you too much, your reality will become based on my perception of events and not your own, which is dangerous. You're right about the dogs. And the other creature was a bull-bear. This is Hatari Forest. We live right outside of it. I am your father, and we came here—,"

"…to make money," Charles finished.

Isra smiled. "Exactly. How?"

"We...you...you!" It all started rushing in. "You're the guardian of the forest! You keep it safe from the dogs and bulls and whatever else is in here. And the town pays you."

"What town?"

"Our town. The one we live in...and the one on the other side that most people haven't been to."

"Good job, Charles. I think you'll be okay. We're almost there. Now, *how* did you fall asleep?"

Charles started to hear the soothing humming again. He could imagine all of the colors he had once seen. It felt like so long ago. Then he remembered the berries. They were so sweet. He couldn't help but taste them. Maybe the berries had put him to sleep. He would have to be careful in the future.

"The berries. There were glowing berries. I started eating them, and then I fell asleep."

"Yes!!! Okay, Charles. You're going to be okay."

Isra stood Charles up and lightly massaged the boy's jaw. Charles winced and grabbed his wrists.

"Hmhm. I may have broken it," Isra said flippantly. "Beckoning Berries, Charles. They got you so fast; I don't even think you heard my warning. All throughout the forest, these berries glow in the presence of life. They're extremely delicious and extremely dangerous. They have the power to hypnotize you. And once you taste them, you begin to forget. Small things at first, but the more you eat, the more you forget. I punched you as soon as I noticed that you were trying to swallow the berries. Sometimes a shock to the system helps. I thought maybe I could knock the berries out of your mouth as well."

Isra opened up his palm to reveal several tiny white pills. Charles reached for one and felt that it was not a pill. It was a tooth. His tooth. He looked up at Isra, mortified. He felt around the inside of his mouth with his tongue and noticed the spaces in between his teeth that had not previously been there. He started to cry.

"Charles. CHARLES. Stop the ridiculous tears. I saved your life. The collateral damage was minimal. You remember eating the berries, and now you know what they can do. The next time you see them, you won't be so susceptible to their allure. Most folks, if they're lucky enough not to get lost in the woods and devoured by shark dogs after they eat the berries, come across the fruits again and have no recollection of ever eating them. It becomes a vicious cycle of indulgence. Pretty soon the amnesia progresses into delirium, and Hatari consumes them, one way or another."

Charles wiped his eyes and tried to quiet his sniffling. He grabbed his bow from the ground and spat out what happened to be mostly blood and partly saliva. He looked up into his father's eyes as he wiped his own.

"What now?" he asked.

"We've made good progress. We should soon be in the middle of the forest. There will be more creatures along the way. Your life will be endangered, but by the time we leave, you will be that much more prepared to be the new guardian of Hatari Forest."

Isra looked up and determined their next steps by the alignment of the stars in the sky. The two journeyed on, shrouded by the deep cover of night.

***

Miles later and deep into the forest, Charles began to droop. His legs grew heavy. His vision became blurry, his throat as dry as the brush upon which he and his father marched. Isra noticed Charles beginning to lag and sat him down against a great tree. He produced a canteen from inside his jacket from which he allowed Charles to drink.

"You're tired. You can't allow the forest to beat you. It doesn't take a creature or anything magical to end your life in this place. The forest itself will bleed you dry of all the will you have to live, if you let it."

Charles drank slowly and only half listened to his father. He was so tired; focusing was difficult. He thought about his mother back at the cabin and Nate, too. He thought about his warm bed. He wished he was home.

"Charles. Charles, you're not listening." Isra slapped the canteen out of Charles's hand and pounced on him, pinning him to the ground.

"You will *die* in this forest!!!" he screamed. Charles was frightened, but he was too worn down to show it. His limbs were limp. He tried to use his eyes to plead with his father for peace. Isra produced a small, sharp knife from within his coat. He held it up to Charles's throat.

"If I sliced you open right now and walked away...how would you survive? How would you dress the wound? How would you prevent the creatures that lust for the smell of blood in the air from devouring you and licking your bones clean? You know NOTHING. And you're here, tired, unfocused, giving up."

Isra grabbed Charles's left arm and held it out to the side. He kept Charles pinned down by pressing his knee into the boy's chest. He pressed the blade into Charles's arm, the pressure growing by the second until blood started to trickle from where the blade sat.

"Maybe this will wake you up. Dress this wound. If you dress it wrong, or too slowly, you have no chance of making it out of this forest."

Isra began to plunge the blade but paused. He turned his ear to the wind. Charles, though stupefied at this point, heard the sound as well. It was a faint screaming, a pitiful, mournful moan, full of anguish. And then the galloping. It was only one horse...at first. That's probably why Isra didn't recognize the sound in time. The horse clipped Isra in passing, knocking him off of Charles onto his back and driving one of its hooves into Isra's arm as it continued running past. Isra yelled out in pain. The impact from the stomp had broken his left arm clean, just above the elbow. Charles raised himself up drowsily and crawled over to Isra, who was writhing in pain. He breathed hard in short thrusts.

"Banshee...horses...st-...st-"

Charles could feel it coming. The damp earth beneath them began to vibrate and then rumble. It sounded like rolling thunder, but Charles knew better. Nothing was that simple in Hatari Forest. He got up and tugged Isra onto his feet. They began to make their way through the forest, but couldn't manage more than a quick trot. The screaming was louder now. It filled their eardrums until they couldn't even distinguish the sound of their feet hitting the ground. Screaming and thunder. Thunder and screaming. They both picked up the pace as a natural reaction to the feeling that something grave was about to take place. Charles sneaked a look behind him as they carried on and saw a thousand red eyes piercing through the dark night, focused on him.

The banshee horse was the oldest race of beast in Hatari Forest. An enigmatic cross between specter and brute, the horses could appear and stampede out of thin air and be gone just as quickly. Nearly every piece of lore about the forest mentioned a traveler seeing, or at least thinking they had seen these beasts. Men and women were found trampled to death in the stories, bones shattered and broken under metallic hooves, with no trace whatsoever that any animal had passed through the area. Legend had it that the albino horses with silver hair and red eyes screamed the last screams of the people who had died beneath them. All the fear, pain, and misery that accompanied a painful death underfoot of the brooding hoard was eternally echoed by each horse, trumpeting the anguish of their victims with every run.

Charles and Isra had dived to the side and out of the stampede path just in time to watch the band of horses race by. Isra nursed his arm that now stung and burned, as if the hoof print was seared into his skin, along with the pain typical of a broken bone. Charles heaved heavily. He wasn't sure how much longer he could make it. As Isra led him deeper and deeper into the forest and away from the horses, he heard his father say, "Almost there." He hoped that in the next town there would be an inn in which he could rest. The trip had taken quite a toll on him, and he was ready for it to be over.

They came into a small clearing with a tiny pond. There was a carpenter's table set up. Charles was immediately confused. A wave of anxiety rushed over him. He fell back a couple of steps behind Isra and surveyed the clearing once more. The pond was bubbling, and a putrid smell arose from it. He turned around and looked into the woods. He didn't know which direction was which, or from where he and his father had come. He was startled to return his gaze to Isra and find him looking directly back at him.

"We only have a little more to go, but the most dangerous part is up ahead. I'll need your bow."

Charles was a much more skilled marksman with a bow than a gun, and much more skilled with a bow than his father to boot. He was hesitant to give up his weapon. The air was so cold, and the smell from the pond was nearly choking him at this point.

"Where are we? What's wrong with that pond?"

"I need your bow," said Isra. He started to approach the bow slowly, his right arm   outstretched in anticipation of the inevitable. Charles was nervous. He took his bow off his back, but he continued to walk backward for each step that his father took toward him. After he took his fifth step back, he hoisted his bow, loaded an arrow, and aimed at Isra's heart. The man stopped walking toward Charles. Charles held his ground.

"My son," Isra said between coughs.

"What is going on here?! Where are we? I...I'll shoot this. I will."

Isra continued to walk toward Charles. Charles had made a good showing, but he couldn't back it up. Isra grabbed the bow softly and angled it down, away from his own vital organs. Then he knelt down to Charles's level and pried every one of his fingers off of the bow before standing up again. In a way, Charles was relieved. He wouldn't have to make the decision between shooting his father or not. There are only so many decisions one can make without power in this world. Charles looked into his father's eyes before Isra turned to continue walking toward the pond. He saw in them peace, poise, something gentle. After walking about ten yards away, Isra turned and aimed the bow at Charles, arrow loaded. Before Charles could fully recognize his predicament, he felt his arrow pierce his leg, right below the kneecap. He knew that it was his arrow because he had fashioned the tips to create a star-shaped entry wound, allowing each point of the star to grip the flesh once the arrow had settled into the body. It was nearly impossible to remove the arrows without tearing out chunks of flesh. Charles knew what he was faced with. He knew he couldn't escape.

"This was the only way," said Isra. "I will die soon, Son. And you, you are not fit to lead the family. For years, I've lured men into this forest and dragged them to their demise." Isra looked back over his shoulder at the bubbling pond. "The acidic pond holds all my secrets. I know I am Hell-bound. I'm a murderous thief who has betrayed his home. I've killed my brethren, my townspeople. I hope God sees that I would have rather burned in

48

Hell than watch my family starve. But you. No. It was never the plan for you to get the inheritance, for you to become the man of the household. You're not ready. And you never will be. You don't have what it takes. I'm sorry, Son. But I have to do this. Your mother and Nathaniel will fare better without you. And besides...you know far too much now."

Isra reached down and grabbed Charles by the neck, hoisting him up. The boy's eyes bulged out of his head. His body hung limp in his father's arms. Isra bent down and lifted Charles onto his shoulder. He turned and slowly approached the acidic pond. The closer they got, the more treacherous the smell climbing out of the pit into the night air became. Charles heard the screaming of the banshee horses in the distance, a baseline to the percussion of the shark dogs' cackling. They were right at the edge of the pond. Isra stood over it with Charles on his shoulders, the shaman of Hatari, prepared to make his final sacrifice.

"I've seen a hundred men die in this caustic pond. Now, I lay to rest my son. My greatest mistake."

Charles felt himself leaning over slowly toward the pond. The weight of his father was pushing with solid force toward the bubbling abyss. Although steady, the fall was very relaxed. With the pond just a few feet away, Charles pondered: *Is Dad falling too?* Charles made a springing motion over his father's shoulder, in an effort to climb down his back. To his surprise, no hands caught or restrained him. He bounded across his father's shoulders and rolled down his back, past his ankles and onto the ground once more. He landed very near the repugnant pond, and its smell burned his eyes and nose so strongly as he hit the ground that he rolled away from the shore as fast as he could. After rolling he got up to his feet. He looked down at his father's body in shock.

Face down in the pool, sinking deeper every moment, was the body of Isra Peregrine. Three arrows stuck tip first out of his back. They had pierced his torso with perfect precision. The acid ate away at the mass of Isra like a hungry pack of hyenas. He dematerialized in front of Charles's very eyes, the pond gurgling and bubbling more than ever, a hungry cauldron of doom.

Across the pond amongst the trees, Charles saw something moving. The figure darted back and forth among the trees, a streak of white amidst the eerie darkness. Finally, it emerged into a small clearing just on the opposite shore of the pond Charles was on. It was a person. A little girl.

Vega Piper.

You see, Vega had told a tiny lie that night not so long ago when Aristotle Piper was lured unsuspectingly and cast into the acidic pool deep within Hatari Forest. She hadn't sat and cried as her father entered the darkness to meet his fate; she had followed him. All night she had stealthily stalked her father and another man as they wound through the paths within the forest. They were attacked by a bull-bear and had a close encounter with a tigress. Vega had watched the man with her father shoot the tigress down with two quick arrows between the eyes. She resolved there in the night to train herself in archery, as it had proved a useful skill.

Vega watched each part of their journey in succession, keeping a watchful eye over her father all the way. She heard the arguing once the men had stopped in the clearing with the acidic pond. She heard the man cry out to her father that there was no town on the other side of Hatari Forest. She watched him abuse her father, and strip him naked of his clothes, money, and belongings. She watched up until the man threw her father's battered body into the pool, which swallowed the shopkeeper down like a pet eager for a treat. She had to turn her head for that part. But right before he was dropped, her father had given Vega all she needed. A name.

His last words were, "Isra, please."

Vega had raced through the forest, crying, tripping, and falling, still in shock. She had no idea where she was going, but she ran miles and miles for hours until she broke out of the woods into a great field. She looked up and saw a cabin, a shed, and a man chopping and stacking wood, a typical early morning chore. The man was Isra Peregrine. She could smell the fumes from the acidic pool radiating off of his body, even from afar. Having found her bearings, she raced two miles east to her home, rushed inside, sat on her bed, and let the shock of the night's events consume her. Amid the hysteria, though, she vowed to avenge the death of her father, one way or another.

Vega had found her way over to the shore on the side of the pond where Charles knelt. They looked each other in the eyes as Isra's legs and feet were slowly pulled into the pond. Charles began to cry, and Vega embraced him. The tears stopped flowing after a few moments, and Charles wiped his face with his coat sleeves. When he looked back toward the pool, Isra was gone. Charles stood up, and Vega put his arm around her shoulder as she helped him to walk.

"Nice shot," he said.

Vega half-smiled.

"C'mon. I know a shortcut from here."

Charles walked home with his guardian, slow and steady. They watched the blood-red sun rise over top the trees of Hatari as the screwbeaks circled overhead. When they reached the field inside the tall grass behind Charles's cabin, Vega turned to go. Charles grabbed her hand, and from his pocket, produced his marble. He clasped it into her hand tautly, his hand trembling as he fought to hold back the tears. Vega wanted to cry too, but she hugged Charles and left before the tears came. Charles stared at his family cabin from the edge of the woods, a home that he had left so recently but that felt so distant to him now. He looked down at where he had broken the arrow   in half that was lodged in his leg, blood and pus crusting over at the entry point of the wound. He checked his quiver and noticed he still had a few arrows. He limped toward the cabin, choked with anxiety, the once-familiar home looking more and more like the forest with each step.

Best Friends

"Gardening is an exercise in optimism. Sometimes, it is a triumph of hope over experience." - Marina Schinz

I'm guilty.

I've been setting women up, lying to them, building each one a glass castle of untruth with my right hand and beckoning the wrecking ball in the distance with my left. I am not a good man.

But I am a good friend.

I've been best friends with Clive Hollow for fifteen years, ever since we started high school. His name is the first thing that strikes you; it's almost like his folks knew he'd be infamous. "Hollow Man"—the playboy, the godsend, the wrecking ball. For all fifteen years that I've known Clive, he's been breaking women's hearts; and not only have I been enabling him, I've been aiding and abetting. Every woman I ever wanted ended up wanting Clive. Every woman he ever had leaned on me to get through to him. And from some weak, jealous place within me, I felt the need to let them fall. Halfway hurt that I couldn't experience even a moment of the happiness he did with these women, and my pride broken from going unchosen, I delivered them right to doom's door by way of the road to destruction. And I never felt remorseful. And Clive never loved a woman.

Until now.

We met Ashley Phoenix when we were nineteen years old. She was twenty-two, or maybe twenty-three. Either way, she was older than us, which only added to her appeal. I knew she wasn't looking at me. Even though going to the library was my idea, and

I had been the one summarizing Alexander Pope's *Essay on Criticism* too loudly for the cramped aisle, I could tell she was looking right through me. Right to Clive.

You see, after years of being friends with Clive, you start to realize a few things:

1. You are not attractive.
2. You don't know how to talk to women.
3. You don't need to know how to talk to women when you're with Clive, and you don't have to worry about being attractive, because the women can't see you. You are invisible.

Clive was the sort of friend you could save from drowning at the beach, and the news would run the story from the angle that the city should be thankful that Clive Hollow escaped a potential watery grave. He was the type of guy who showed up late and empty-handed, but got the best seat in the house and the coldest brew. I wouldn't be surprised if people sang him happy birthday on *their* birthdays, just to make him feel special. You just wanted him to like you, you know? You didn't really know why, but it seemed important that he like you.

Ashley Phoenix walked right past me and up to Clive. He was more than a foot taller than she was, and so anytime she looked up to make eye contact, to the unknowing, it looked like she was pleading. Maybe it was foreshadowing.

She used some corny pick-up line; I had never heard a girl use a pick-up line on a guy. She seemed so...regular. Ironically, the fact that she was unremarkable in many ways was exactly what made her fit so well with Clive. She was a good person, but her head was never too far in the clouds. She was always within reach. She didn't require chasing. He took to her easily, naturally, like roots to soil. Throughout their time together, if anything could ground Clive and make him feel stable, it was her. She made him strong and provided him with the lessons and experiences he needed to grow into a better man.

But we never really think about how the soil feels when the plant is plucked. We imagine how happy the blossom may make someone, or how its graduation from the dirt is joyous, only until we remember that this new life is simply the beginning of death. But we never think about the soil. Precious soil. How does it feel to nurture something, to put your all into it every day of your life, and all at once watch it taken away from you forever? When planting season comes again, do you yearn for the one you lost, so long ago? Does your generosity abound? Or do you grow increasingly weary with the coming and going of each harvest season, nothing to show for your unconditional selflessness?

But, whatever.

The beginning was good, like it always is. They had ups and downs, but their bond grew strong very rapidly. If you can imagine a solitary tree, swaying and bending under hurricane winds, you can imagine the perseverance (or naïve determination) of their relationship. Evident from all the on-and-off dating, they couldn't stay away from each other. Ashley was a purposeful under-achiever, according to Clive. Based on where she started, she probably could have graduated with her master's in clinical psychology by the time we met her. She had taken one fall semester off for financial reasons and had an awakening. Why would she pay to learn, when knowledge was free all around her? By utilizing her network, public libraries, and the Internet, nearly anything could be self-taught. She wasn't paying for an education; she was paying for a siphon. You see, the educational system in America was just a microcosm of the systematic oppression that had been crippling the minorities in the nation since its birth. It was a matter of the wealthy and privileged having more access to the blah, blah, blah, blah, blah, blah...

Blah.

She never really took the effort to teach herself anything. Realizing she didn't have to lean on "the powers that be" for her enlightenment was as far as she needed to go to be comfortable.

From ages twenty-one to twenty-three, she had taken one class a semester, eventually un-enrolling to get more hours at work. Some summers she took a couple of classes, but she missed so many days (summer was her prime travel period) that she got no credit for them. But she was smart. She had a pretty good job, and nobody could tell her that she wasn't smart. And most days, that was enough.

Clive had played out his Lacrosse scholarship to the max of his eligibility at State, and along with his personality, a starting spot on a perennial Division I LAX powerhouse team didn't make it easy for Clive or anybody else to pretend that he didn't have the attention of women. Many women. He and Ashley fought most times over things related to groupies or side-relationships and their emotional depth. But Clive had never told Ashley he was ready to be her "boyfriend"—a wave of a loophole that he rode toward a never-nearing shore. And though the roots never took complete hold in the soil, the climate was such that collaboration on a sturdy crop was born. Ashley made Clive a better man; and as many mistakes as he made, he never quit trying to make her happy. I've known Clive Hollow since we were fifteen years old, and the only woman he's ever admitted to loving is Ashley Phoenix.

I remember the first conversation I had with Ashley as a relationship arbitrator. But to fully understand the significance of that, you have to know the gist of how similar conversations went with droves of Clive's women in the past.

I had always been the perfect diversion. I wasn't necessarily encouraging to the women who thought they could win Clive's heart back (as if they really ever had it), but I gave them just enough hope to keep their boats afloat. Misdirection was the name of the game. Ambiguity? Par for the course. I was a professional, an all-star. All-Decepticon First Team, starting center, leading the league in blocks. Unthreatening-seemingly-trustworthy-best-friend-atron. Or something like that. Let's use Kim, one of the last girls Clive dated before Ashley, as an example.

Me: So...you have a boyfriend, and he treats you right?

Kim: Yes, his name is George.

Me: Hm. Okay. But you're in love with Clive?

Kim: Yes.

Me: And your boyfriend knows this?

Kim: He knows enough. He knows that Clive is the love of my life, and as soon as he's ready to have me, I'll drop everything and come running.

Me: Well then. It's uh, great that you all have an understanding.

Kim: Yeah, I guess. But can I ask you something?

Me: Ask away (translation: No).

Kim: Do you think...oh gosh...do you think I'll ever really have a chance with Clive? Like does he talk about me ever? Has he ever said anything to give you the idea that I could be the one for him?

Me: [*With an Oscar award-winning tone and delivery*] You know what, Kim? Clive and I have been friends for a long time. The way he looks at you, I can tell...you're special. You have a lot going on with your relationship and school and all, and Clive isn't the guy that's going to distract you from those things. He's not selfish. Whatever he feels the potential is between you all, he's going to keep it to himself, because he doesn't see it as his place to just come along and change your life around. So, if you want more of Clive, you're going to have to make some changes. But you have to be careful. If he gets the sense you're altering your life just for him and it doesn't feel organic, it's not going to work. He's all about "the feel" in situations like this. (Translation: No).

Lights dim. Curtain closes. The crowd goes wild.

I had literally left her with no option but to continue enabling the status quo. The opponent was successfully frozen, my best friend saved yet again from certain calamity, unbeknownst to him. I'd like to thank God, my mama, and the academy. Score one for the home team. My friend was happy, so I was happy. Until Ashley.

"I just don't know what to do with him. He says he's not ready, but it's been three years," she said. "I'm thinking he'll never be ready. He's making a conscious decision not to give me his all because he knows I won't go anywhere. He's got me wrapped around his finger. I keep telling him I'll leave one day, and one day I will. But I don't want it to come to that...so...I guess that's why I called you. I've just...been trying to make sense of it all. And figure out...I don't know...if he even cares about me, I guess."

Now, I could have very well given Ashley the script I had given so many times. I could have steered her mind away from the imminent danger posed by the gold-plated barbed wires that signify Clive Hollow's allure. It would have been easy. There were things Clive didn't like about Ashley. The fact that she wouldn't finish school was a big one. Her complacency scared him, made him think a life with only her would inevitably be a sentence of twenty-five to life of boring consistency. She had a good body but not a great body. There may have been a more attractive version of her out in the world somewhere; who knows? I could have manipulated her flaws in such a way that left her in a desert of self-doubt and insecurity, reinforcing that the only oasis was her relationship with Clive. This would also reinforce the idea that the best move was no move at all. Just keep the lights on. Just keep the show going.

But I was always the guy who had to wait. I was always boyfriend No. 2, or an aspiring boyfriend; I was good enough to send you flowers, but not quite good enough to be seen with you in public. I was jealous of Clive, and I wanted Ashley. It wasn't so much *her* I wanted as it was someone like her. I wanted someone to love me so hard that there would be nothing I could do to get rid of her. I was certain that if that situation ever presented itself, there was nothing I *would* do to push someone away. So I empathized. I felt Ashley's pain and saw, for the first time, the true fallout Clive's actions had on others. So I sold him out. But, not in a spiteful way. It just seemed...

...right?

"Ashley. I've known Clive most of my life, and I've never seen him look at anyone the way he looks at you. I've never heard him talk about anybody the way he talks about you. Usually, I'm the first non-family member invited when holiday dinner is ready. This year, you opened the door when I pulled into the driveway.

He's never cried to any women about his problems. Real tears. His mother and sister have never taken any other woman to church with them. There have been plenty of women...but you're the only woman he's ever told me he's loved."

Ashley cried. Half were probably tears of joy, the other half, confusion. We got closer that day. I couldn't just write her off like I could every other woman, and she could trust me to be honest with her. We talked often and had many more conversations like that first one. We became friends. Ironically, Clive was ecstatic about the change; we got to hang out more because we could do things in threes instead of twos. After "the conversation," as I like to call it, I lived in constant fear that my betrayal of Clive's system would come back to haunt me. That I would slide down the slippery slope of "doing the right thing" into the pit of no return: chronic do-goodism.

It only took a year.

My exact words were, "Sometimes, you have to let go." I tried a thousand times to tell myself that it wasn't that particular sentence that broke Clive and Ashley up. I analyzed all the connotations and inferences and assumptions that could be derived from that phrase, and I pretended like I did it so I would have a defense when Clive questioned me. But really I did it because I was guilty. Clive and Ashley broke up, and my palms sweated anytime I was around him. When either of their names would show up on my phone, my heart would skip a beat. I couldn't sleep, so I spent most nights consoling one or the other of them. To this day, it's the worst breakup I've ever gone through, and it wasn't even mine.

Ashley called me one night crying over Clive—the usual. About how he wasn't ready, and the other women, and the lying, and the lack of progress. Ashley and I were always very candid with each other, but I had also tried to soften the blows I had to give her when it came to Clive. But that night? It seemed like we chased our tails for hours. I tried to explain that a man will tell and show you exactly who he is—early on, too. We're really not good liars. We're only good at being confusing. We might act differently than we speak or speak differently than we act so that you can't discern what's true or not, but patterns are undeniable.

Clive had been cheating on Ashley the entire time they were together. He'd wake up Sunday morning and put her on a plane home from his college town, kiss her good-bye at the airport, and call me about some Navy chick or volleyball girl or chemistry professor who he fucked later on that night. I never felt sorry for Ashley—because she knew all of this. She had made every excuse for him she could: youth, long distance, convenience. She had caught him; he had admitted it several times, and I used to wonder *what else do you need*? But then again, I'd never been in love. I didn't realize at the time that love grants unconditional and inexplicable rights to remain in a fucked up situation. But believe me, I know now.

So she asked me, "What should I do?" And I told her something that I truly believe. I told her what I thought every time

Clive or Ashley called me to complain about the other. I told her that my mother never cared about looking out for me until child services took me to my first foster home—then she always wanted to visit. I told her that sometimes you have to disappear to become fully visible. I told her that sometimes you have to let go. You have to do what's best for you, or else you'll always be living your life waiting on someone else, trying to become their picture of perfection, and that's a fate much more tragic than any lost love.

Even still, it took another year. I stopped talking to Ashley as much. Clive too. Everybody really—I was finishing up my MBA and trying to find employment. We never really grew apart in my mind; time just kind of froze. I knew that Clive and Ashley had been doing their usual on-and-off even after "the second conversation." The intervals in between commitments varied. But two weeks ago, Clive called me infuriated, saying Ashley had another boyfriend. He sobbed on the phone as I tried to console him, tried to make my words the glue that mends broken hearts, but I knew it was futile. I have been reaching out to Ashley, but she still won't respond to my texts or calls. Clive has called me every day for two weeks either screaming or crying about Ashley. Most people won't feel bad for Clive, and I can't blame them. They'll call it "just desserts" or "a taste of his own medicine," which is mostly true.

But I have no choice except to feel remorseful. Without my part in this, maybe his heart never gets broken. You'd have to see him to understand. It's pitiful. Sadly pitiful. If you could only imagine the moment Lucifer was cast from Heaven, his body colliding painfully with the ground below. I imagine that he looked up toward the sky, the surreal nature of his situation overwhelming him and inducing a state of shock, which was probably followed by a fit of emotion. How the tears must have fallen as he came to terms with the gravity of his new reality. Do you know how it feels to lose everything? How could anything other than resentment and vengeance well up inside of him for the rest of his days? I'm scared for what's to become of my friend. What's wild is the conversations with Clive about letting go and moving on and respecting what people express to you are eerily similar to the ones I used to have with Ashley. They really are made for each other. But not right now.

I guess I'm just confused about what friendship means now. I've been doing a lot of soul-searching—even started journaling again. I jumped in front of a bullet for a woman who would never be mine. Then I gave her the hammer she used to break my best friend's heart. I can't tell you if I've been a friend to either Clive or Ashley. I used to think I was in the middle to make things better, but I may have been doing the opposite. Maybe I don't know as much as I thought I did. I feel so guilty. I want to grow from this, but I don't know how. I don't think my life has been arable for quite some time. I guess I'll just have to be patient. We'll all have to be patient and wait for our next chance to blossom.

April 4, 2012

S.J

Big Redd Writing 'Hood

Oh, it was a bright day. The sun had crept up into the sky while all of Purr-lem was sleeping. By the time the cocks got up to crow, a new day had dawned. On the west side of the city, though, hunched over his desk, pen in paw, one cool cat had been awake for hours. He was writing a research report on one of the baddest jazz cats who ever lived, Cat Basie. It wasn't due until Monday, but our friend was so passionate about the topic, he had awakened in the wee hours of the morning and set himself immediately to finishing the report.

He found that he was most creative during the quiet parts of the day, the parts without the sounds from the hustle and bustle of Purr-lem city life. When he could hear the wind softly whistle in the alleyway outside his window or the first chirps of birds that would later become that day's folly—he was completely at peace. And so he wrote freely, nearly effortlessly, without any interruptions until his family and neighbors yawned and stretched their way into the new day.

Purr-lem was a city on the decline, not yet fallen from grace but hanging from the jagged, slippery rocks of misfortune, the sea of ruin rushing madly down below. Just ten years earlier, Purr-lem had been a cultural anomaly, the "Cat Mecca" of the nation. At one point, nearly ninety percent of its population consisted of cats, and the world's greatest cat dancers, artists, writers, and activists either called the city home or came there often to perform in what was quickly becoming one of the most-renowned hotbeds for artistic talent in the world. Just a decade earlier Cat Basie had graced the stage at venues like The Yarn Ball Club and The Maine Coon Ballroom.

Our hero's arts and culture course at school required that he create a report on a great cultural influence for the city of Purr-lem. Since Cat Basie had grown up in the Florence Mills apartments—the same building in which our friend sat that morning writing vigorously—he had decided to write his report on how growing up in Purr-lem had influenced and shaped his favorite meow-sician's style and sound, and in turn, how the music Cat Basie created told the story of an everyday Purr-lem cat, celebrating a rich history that made regular felines feel like pharaohs.

"Redd! Reeedddddd!!"

The call shook Redd up so much that he dropped his pen. He hadn't heard his mother's first two calls, being so consumed with his work and all. The call he *had* heard startled him—he normally heard his mother wake up, get out of bed, and make her way downstairs to the kitchen, so the suddenness of her beckoning and the distance of her voice had temporarily confused him, or "balled him up" as the kittens say these days.

"Yes, Mama?" Redd asked after he had rushed downstairs.

Mama Eleanor was an American Shorthair, just like her two boys. She had aged gracefully, her face retaining a playful nature and her coat holding on to a youthful shine. She actually cut a funny character in her bonnet and nightgown, which were typically an old lady-cat's accoutrements. In her adolescence, she was known as one of the most beautiful cats in all the land, her silvery fur sparkling under stage lights as she sang. Everybody said she was the "sweetest voice to come out of Purr-lem." But her oldest boy had come out orange-red, with soft, fluffy fur, and the older he got, the redder he got. His fur flourished, and his red streaks and spirals gave him a distinct coat that all Mama Eleanor's friends raved about. His father had been red, so it made sense, I suppose. But seeing her son always reminded her of her lost love, and her playful face would give way to a sad twinkle in her eye, if only for a moment.

"I need you to run to the store and get some milk, we're almost out."

"Okay, Mama."

Redd turned toward the living room to grab some money from his wallet. Their family didn't have much, so he never expected money from his mother when she asked him to run errands. Sometimes he was able to make a little extra change after school carrying groceries for neighbors or watching cars for the businesscats across from city hall. He did whatever he could to help.

"Where are you going, Son? Here, here's a few dollars."

Redd grabbed the money and hurried quickly toward the door.

"Be right back, Mama!"

"Not so fast, mister," said Mama Eleanor in the tone she used when Redd was getting ahead of himself. "I don't want you to go to the market on the corner. I want you to go—"

As she was speaking, her youngest son, Tab, had scurried into the room and jumped on his brother, scratching and biting him playfully. He was a typical, energetic kitten, and he loved his brother more than anything in the world, which, of course, annoyed his brother more than anything in the world.

"Come on, Tab. Beat it, will ya?!"

Mama Eleanor chuckled. She loved seeing her boys together. And with the fact that Tab's coat resembled her own, she remembered the fun she and the boys' father used to have when they were younger when she saw the boys playing together.

"Take your brother with you, Redd."

"Yayyyyyy!!!" Tab squealed.

"Awwww, Mama!"

"And like I was saying, I want you to go to the market downtown, not the one on the corner. The milk is cheaper there, and it's also fresher on Saturday mornings. But I need you to hurry back, because I have to use that milk to start making dinner."

"Okay, Mama." Redd sulked. Tab was struggling to pull on his boots on the floor in front of the door. Redd was halfway in, halfway out of the door waiting for Tab when a thought crossed his mind.

"Mama! You know how busy it is trying to get downtown Saturday morning. If I have to go aaaaaaall that way to get the milk, keeping up with Tab is only going to slow me down. You said you wanted me back quick, right?"

Mama Eleanor pondered. She realized what Redd was doing, but he had a good point. Redd wasn't the most diligent at times, and she'd hate for anything to happen to Tab while they rushed downtown on a Saturday morning.

"Okay, Mr. Big Cat. You have a point. Leave Tab here, but hurry back!"

Redd slid slyly out of the door sticking his tongue out at Tab just as it was closing. He heard an "Awww, Ma!" very similar to his own come from his little brother as the door closed behind him.

The city air bathed Redd as soon as he exited the building. It was inner-city air, so although it wasn't the purest, there was something very refreshing about it for Redd. Every time he was out and about on his own in Purr-lem, he felt like a celebrity. The old cats on the corner would always ask him about his family or how school was going. Sometimes they would call out, "Hey, cat daddy, ya lookin' good," or "Good to see ya, young fella!" as he passed their corners. Before Redd and his family had moved to Purr-lem, his mother was very cautious about where she let him go alone, but the community was so close-knit in Purr-lem that she gave him a little more leeway. He loved the sense of freedom he had walking through city. It energized him so much; he broke into a swift trot.

By the time he saw Zora, he was colliding with her face.

Both of the cats fell backward onto the pavement. Redd arose quickly and tried to help his neighbor up. They stood and looked each other in the eyes.

"Hi, Big Redd," she said.

A couple things here worth mentioning. First, everybody outside of Redd's family called him "Big Redd." Back when his father was around, he had been the original Big Redd. But since it was only Redd and Tab now, the neighborhood called Redd "Big Redd," and Tab "Little Red." This didn't make much sense, especially since Redd wasn't big and Tab wasn't red, but they took the names as terms of endearment and didn't complain. Second, and more important to our story—Redd loved Zora. He had loved her since the moment he first saw her. She was a beautiful Ragdoll, covered in white fluffy fur with a single tan stripe right above her nose. Her eyes were a bright, beautiful blue, and they sparkled in the sunlight. She wore a dainty pendant around her neck of a similar blue color. Her grandmother had given it to her. Now, back to our hero. Things were about to get interesting

"Um, hi. Hello, Zora. I'm sorry for runnin' into ya. It was awful clumsy of me."

"It's no problem. Where are you headed in such a hurry?"

"I gotta go to the store to pick up some things for Mama."

"You're going all alone?" Zora asked, impressed.

"Mhm. I sure am. Say, you wanna come with me? It'll be fun. It's a mighty fine day out."

"Aw, jeez. I wish I could, Redd. But I'm actually about to get started running some errands for my grandmother, maybe next time."

"Oh, okay," said Redd, dejected.

"Yeah, sorry about that. I can't even run my own errands. I had planned to go downtown to the new yarn store. They have these lovely colored yarn balls, and I wanted to pick one up for my friend. Her birthday is coming up, but the party is tomorrow. I'll just have to get her a card instead."

At this moment, our hero saw a chance, and he took it.

"Say, Zora. I'm headed to the market downtown. Why don't I pick up the yarn ball for you and bring it around to you later?"

Her beautiful, diamond eyes sparkled.

"Really?! Aww, would you do that for me. I would appreciate it so much. She's going to love it so much. There's a lavender yarn ball with sparkles in it. That's the one I was going to get."

Zora reached into her pocketbook, but Redd stopped her.

"Don't worry; I got a little extra grocery money. I'll get the yarn. You just worry about your errands. I'll bring the yarn by your house tonight once you're back."

Zora leaned in and licked Redd's cheek. His whole body got warm, and he withheld the urge to purr.

"You're just the sweetest thing. You don't know how much this means to me. I'll see you later. Remember, lavender with sparkles."

"Lavender with sparkles."

Zora smiled and headed on her way. Redd restarted the trot that had led him to collide with Zora. Maybe it was a good luck trot. Either way, this day was getting better and better.

There was so much to see and do in Purr-lem. The sights and sounds of the vibrant neighborhood could entrance anyone. The 'hood was a melting pot of creativity, art, and culture. It seemed like everybody was talented, and because it was cool to be artistic, the community fostered the creative growth and development of young residents, creating a vanguard of artists. Folks would be out on the streets painting, playing instruments, or singing on sunny days like this. The cats who had migrated to Purr-lem from the islands always had fur care products and services with which they tried to win over passersby. Near the island cats was a street cart where Old Randy sold milksicles. He had all different flavors. Redd loved the cool treats on hot days and looked forward to the flavors Old Randy had, which were always changing. He thought today would be a great day to try a coconut-flavored one.

Past the street cart and the subway was a small park where the old cats would play chess. Sometimes Redd would sit nearby and watch the games for a while. The focused old cats hardly ever noticed he was there. The park was an oasis of peace in a rambunctious expanse. Right outside the park, mama cats pulled their sleepy, hissing kittens up and down the block from the laundromat to the corner store to wherever else they needed to go. The high school cats drove up and down the block in their first cars. The gas they used going nowhere was their investment in the affection of any pretty kitty's eyes they might catch.

After the park was the old theater. It was where all the big comedy cats, singers, and dancers came to perform. Redd had gone inside one time to the second floor. Not many cats knew about the second floor where the theater managers would host secret dinners for their honored patrons and performers. When his mother had first stopped singing, they threw her a farewell dinner on the secret floor. Any given day, you could find famous or up-and-coming cats around the theater, or anywhere in Purr-lem really. Big names frequented the neighborhood, if not to perform, to gain inspiration for upcoming projects. Who could blame them? With creativity pulsing through the veins of Purr-lem, the stories told themselves. The famous cats were normally down-to-earth and friendly with the locals. The Purr-lem community was like a family, and even if you were just passing through, you'd be sure to get some love before you left town.

Above all else Redd loved the music. Through all the sounds of the city, it was the music that hypnotized him. Whether it was the teenage cats blasting their radios, the street performers, or music wafting down from open windows high above the street, the music was the heartbeat of the city. It let Redd know that Purr-lem was awake and thriving. He would put an extra pep in his step and groove down the sidewalk or even sing along with the songs he knew. Purr-lem was a busy place for busy people, and sensory overload was much less of a possibility than a certainty. But above all else, Redd heard the music. He always heard the music.

Purr-lem was Redd's carnival. He was having so much fun, he hadn't realized how near he was to the market. He also hadn't noticed just how much time he had taken to get downtown, what with all the milksicles, chess games, catch-up conversations, and such. He frolicked past all of the sights and sounds with the utmost joy. He trotted and skipped and spun and crashed.

Right into Wallace.

He fell backward, dropping his pack, the contents spilling all over the sidewalk. A small toy mouse flopped out of the bag, its eyes sparkling in the sun. It was Redd's favorite toy, his good luck charm, if you will. He carried it with him everywhere. The toy was nothing more than a soft, plush mouse shape with bright, gold-colored beads for the eyes. The body was dirty and frayed in some places, for no child's toy leaves every adventure unscathed. Mama Eleanor had given Redd the toy when he was a tiny kitten, but instead of honing his hunting skills and practicing his predator techniques on the lifeless target, he had considered the mouse his first friend. He carried the toy everywhere, slept next to it, and cried whenever anyone took it away from him. Older cats said Mama Eleanor had given it to him too young. "You're gonna mess the boy up, Eleanor. He'll walk around thinking we're not supposed to catch those vermin," her sister had said. Mama Eleanor watched Redd play with the toy on the floor, purring with content. "He's happy. Let him be," was her response.

Redd scrambled to gather his contents and stuff them back into his pack. Wallace helped him. A tall Abyssinian across the street had noticed the collision and watched with particular interest as Redd stuffed the mouse back into the pack.

"In so big a hurry, for so little a furry. Where you going Big Redd?" Wallace asked.

Wallace was one of the older cats in Redd's neighborhood. He was a teacher by day, and he also did some work with the church. Otherwise, he was an artist. You name it, and he could do it: draw, paint, play instruments. He had played piano for Mama Eleanor in her heyday. They grew up together and were very close. He always tried to look out for Redd when he saw him away from his mother. He was a long, thin Sphynx, with dark-colored skin. He normally wore a bowler hat and small, round, silver-rimmed glasses. His long ears stuck out to either side of his bowler, and he kept a pencil tucked in between the hat and his left ear. He said he often thought of inspiration for art throughout the day and had to jot his ideas down before he forgot them. Wallace was a strange cat; amicable to all, and no one could ever remember seeing him flustered. Sometimes he would stand in front of his porch facing the street until long after the sun had gone down, humming or mumbling, nobody could tell for sure. He always spoke in riddles. Some of the younger cats poked fun at him and called him names. But Redd loved him. And he loved Redd back.

"The store! I have to get milk for Mama. Oh! And the yarn store. I told Zora I would get her some new yarn, so I have to go there first. But then the milk."

"Ah, yes. The lovely Purr-incess Zora. I'm sure she'll be happy with whatever you bring back. And does your mother know that you're making this...detour, shall we call it?"

"Well yeah! Well...no. But it was just a small detour. Just going to grab the yarn real quick, I already know what kind and everything."

"Ah, I see. Well, you're only adding an hour detour to your trip. It's still fairly light out. You should be fine."

"An hour? Isn't the new yarn store downtown? A couple blocks away from the big market?"

"No, no, my friend. They were thinking about putting it there but decided to move it about twelve stops downtown from there. The space was cheaper. Bigger too."

"So...I have to ride the train?" Redd asked timidly. He had never ridden on the train alone before.

"You could walk, my friend. But I guarantee you wouldn't make it back in time for dinner, which I'm assuming your mother needs the milk for either way," Wallace smiled.

"Rats! The dinner! I'm supposed to be hurrying back to get her the milk so she can make dinner. I gotta go, Wallace! You said twelve stops up?!"

"Yes, my fast-moving friend. But I might ask, before you scurry off so furiously. Could you not get the yarn tomorrow? Sweet Mama Eleanor needs that milk. Now I've never been one to discount the power of a generous favor for a pretty kitty, but I wouldn't want you to get in trouble with your mother."

"Aww, shucks. I really like her, Wallace. I thought maybe if I got her the yarn —" Redd hung his head. "I don't know. But I already told her I would get it. I can't turn back now."

"Hm. I see. A cat of his word. Well, just remember; pie is why pussy cats crawl into jails, my friend."

"What do ya mean, Wallace?"

"Purr-haps the allure of sweet things can lead us into dangerous places. You should be extra careful. If you're going to the yarn store, I'd suggest catching the next F train. It leaves in a few minutes. I'll go grab the milk and take it home for you; that way your mother can start dinner for Li'l Redd. Be safe and hurry back. Don't talk to any strange cats."

Redd latched on to Wallace and gave him a huge hug.

"Thank you so much, Wallace."

"No problem, my little friend. Now, beat it. The train will be here soon."

Redd bolted off toward the train stop. Wallace looked after him and smiled, shaking his head. He departed toward the market whistling a tune he had made up in his head earlier. Across the street, the tall Abyssinian cat stealthily followed Redd to the train station.

***

"One ticket downtown, please" Redd asked hesitantly.

"You sure?" the attendant cat laughed nasally.

The ticket was more expensive than he had realized. He would have just enough money to buy the yarn and take a bus home. Just enough. Our hero waited in the cavernous subway for the next train downtown, which the attendant had told him would come in ten minutes. Cats crowded the platform. Some were obviously waiting for trains; others, Redd wasn't so sure about. They jumped and frolicked in the underground area as if it was their playground.

He saw some rough-looking cats standing in the corner, waiting for the same train he was. He knew some of the older cats had starting hanging in tough clowders. Some of the ones he grew up with left school and started getting into trouble around the neighborhood. Mama Eleanor had told him and Tab that a decade or so earlier, everybody was too occupied with making art and having fun to cause any trouble. But coming out on the other side of the depression, the city had lost its glowing allure for many cats. They needed money and jobs. Life got hard. And the new stress was unraveling Purr-lem from the core, starting with the youth.

The train came, and Redd crowded in with the commuters. Even though he was small, there was no space for him to sit on the train. He didn't mind. He figured if he sat, some of the bigger cats might challenge him to move before the ride was over anyway. The air was muggy and smelled like tuna. Usually Redd loved tuna, but not this time. He crouched in a corner and leaned up against the back wall of the train, so he wouldn't fall when it stopped abruptly. The ride was far from peaceful. Some of the street cats were dancing, singing, and swinging on the poles in the subway train. The clowder cats cursed and laughed loudly, standing in the middle of the car. There were also families of cats in the car; mama, papa, and kitties. Some laughed heartily all scrunched together. Others looked annoyed until they had a chance to exit the train.

Redd hadn't realized how fatigued he felt until he began crouching in the corner. His day was an odyssey for such a small cat. The muggy heat started feeling soothing, and the noise from the commuters became an ambient drone that worked to hypnotize him. Redd knew better than to fall asleep. His brain told him: *Stay awake. Don't drift to sleep. You can't go to sleep.* But Redd's eyelids slid farther and farther over his eyes, as the horizon slides over the sun with the ending day. It wasn't until the door he had fallen asleep leaning against opened up and he spilled out of the train car that he awakened.

Last stop Downtown. Next train uptown leaves in 15 minutes.

Redd scurried out of the train worriedly and bolted upstairs to the attendant.

"Where am I?"

"All the way downtown, moe. Furhall Street."

Redd ran out of the station and onto the street. He had only missed the yarn store by one stop, which relieved him a bit, but he would have to walk. The sun was setting, and Redd wasn't quite sure which direction he should go in, but he knew he was only off by a block. He decided to walk toward the sun. He remained hopeful that Wallace had been able to get the milk for his mother. He knew that even if she got the milk, he would be in trouble. He was supposed to be the one to bring it, and fast. As the shadows grew like weeds on the pavement, he started to understand the craziness Wallace had said about pies and jails.

Redd looked up and saw a wide building with massive windows in the distance. Outside the front entrance, a metal ball of yarn rotated like the Earth.

Yarn World.

Redd raced toward the building. His legs could carry him but only so fast. As he approached the front door though, he slowed. His legs and his heart grew heavy. The building was cold and sterile inside. Creaking sounds from the spinning yarn orb were the only indications of life in the entire vicinity. A massive parking lot devoid of vehicles, a million non-luminous lights, Yarn World was closed. Our hero was too late. Redd sat on the pavement facing the entrance to the building and began to weep.

With his face in his paws, he didn't notice the clowder of cats begin to surround him. The sun had dropped below the cityscape, so the marauders cast no shadow as they stealthily slid out of the alleys and stood over Big Redd. All of a sudden, Redd felt himself lifted high into the air. When the acceleration upward came to a quick halt, the sensation of gravity pulling him quickly toward the pavement took over his body. He twisted and turned in the air, stretching and flailing his paws out of instinct. He landed on his feet, but hard. His left paw jolted, causing him to screech and stumble a few steps.

"What do we have here?"

The tall Abyssinian cat who had stalked Redd earlier stood over him now, holding his backpack high in the air. An extremely tall cat, he wore dark sunglasses and golden hoop earrings. The fur atop his head was particularly fluffy, and his body was mostly gray with black tiger stripes. Redd knew him; his name was Bo. Bo was one of the toughest cats in the neighborhood. He had dropped out of school, joined a clowder, and started robbing cats in other neighborhoods. Eventually, his troublemaking had caught up with him, and he had spent some time in a jail upstate. There were rumors in Purr-lem that he had come home, but most cats weren't sure. The truth is that Bo had been home for months, keeping a low profile. He had reconnected with his girlfriend, Jo, who looked like a yellow female replica of him, and he started his own clowder from cats he used to run with and some of the up-and-coming bad cat-titudes in the neighborhood.

One of the clowder cats pinned Redd down on the pavement.

"I don't know, babe, what do we have?" asked Jo.

"Some runt. I saw him talking to crazy ol' Wallace earlier."

Bo turned Redd's backpack upside down and let the contents spill all over him. Redd's mouse toy dropped out last, hit Redd in the face as he looked up, and bounced onto the pavement.

"Claw-some. *That's* exactly what I was looking for. How kind of you to come all the way downtown alone, just so I could take it from you with no trouble. Paws-itively genius, little guy."

Bo's cronies laughed the way cronies laugh when the leader makes a dumb joke. Bo picked up the mouse toy and examined it.

"Mhmm. These are some pretty eyes. Almost as pretty as yours, babe."

Jo swooned watching her bad boy in control. "Bet we can get a nice payout from that one, huh sweetie?"

"Maybe. It's a little worn. Looks like the little brat's been playing around with it. Dumb kittens. Can't appreciate the finer things in life. Either way, I'm sort of fond of this one. I think I might keep it regardless."

Bo smiled to show one front tooth missing amongst the row of sharpened others. Redd's blood was boiling. He watched as Bo slid the mouse toy into his coat pocket. Redd started shaking furiously and, in a flash, darted from beneath the paw of his oppressor. The entire clowder braced themselves, surprised at his escape. Redd crouched in a predatory stance and evaluated the scenario. There were four cats in the clowder, not including Bo and Jo. They stood in a semicircle with Bo and Jo just outside the helm, protecting their leader. The cats who had braced themselves soon eased their tensions and began to laugh at their previous thought that Redd could pose any threat. Amidst all the laughter, Redd let out a furious screech followed by a venomous hiss.

"This little brat wants a fight? You gotta be lion." Bo said. "Do you know who you're messing with? Run home to your mommy, kid. The toy is mine."

As Bo and Jo turned to walk away, Redd maneuvered in between the legs of the clowder members and leaped on to Bo's neck. He started scratching furiously before Bo shook him off. He couldn't catch his balance this time. Redd hit the ground on his back and had barely touched the pavement when the entire clowder was upon him, clawing and biting him ferociously.

Redd screamed and hissed, but all of the cats were much bigger than he was. The onslaught of bites and scratches momentarily subsided as he watched Bo hover over him. Bo smiled his gap-toothed smile before pawing Redd in the face, over and over. Redd got weaker and weaker. He closed his eyes and tried to make himself go numb.

All of a sudden, the pawing stopped. Redd flattened out on the pavement from exhaustion. Through watery eyes, he saw Bo fly over him and hit the ground on the other side with a thud. The clowder rushed over to Bo and surrounded him. Redd sat up to see Wallace and three other counselors from the Cats & Kitties club of Purr-lem. Wallace had a long wooden cane with him, the head of which was the head of Bastet. His bowler and glasses remained unmoved. In his calm, collected voice, he spoke in short, per usual.

"Party's over, cool cats. You fellas get home safe, alright?"

The clowder of cats hissed and sneered. Bo stood up, aided by Jo, and glared at Wallace and the counselors. He looked down at Redd and hissed, "This isn't over." And with that, the clowder dispersed into the shadows as stealthily as they had arrived.

Redd struggled to stand up and looked Wallace in the eye.

"Wallace, I—"

"Let's go home, Big Redd." Wallace interrupted, smiling. "Let's go home. We'll talk about it tomorrow."

Wallace put Redd on his back and walked toward his car with the counselors. Redd nestled into Wallace's warm back and tried to ignore the aches in his body. He was asleep before they even got to the car.

***

In conclusion, growing up in Purr-lem wasn't easy for Cat Basie. Even though the city inspired him to be a great musician, he was challenged each day to keep his integrity, as many of us are. His dedication to his art and the support of his community were the saving graces that kept Basie out of trouble and moving fur-ward. So when we hear him play now, it's not just a song of jubilee. It is a song of triumph, perseverance. His sound shows us everything we are, and everything we hope to become. We hear how far we have come and dream of how far we will one day go.

Redd took his seat in the middle of the class as the clapping of his peers subsided. "Great job, Big Redd," one of his catmates leaned over and said. Redd smiled. He looked out of the window. It was a beautiful, sunny day outside. He couldn't wait to take the walk home. Redd closed his eyes and imagined breathing in that freedom air. It wouldn't be long now. He could almost hear the music.

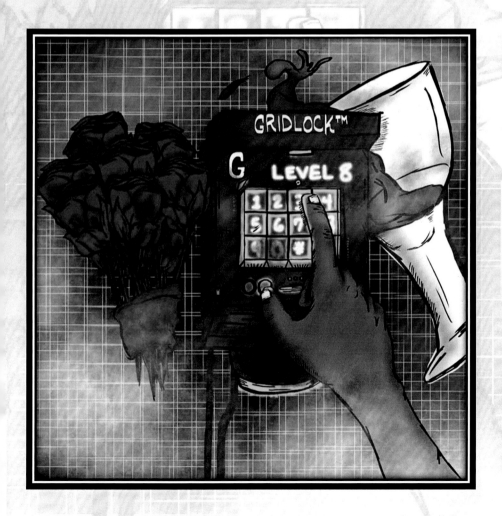

I don't like Daryl.

I never did. When my sister brought him home, I thought he was a pretentious, pretty-boy asshole, and I don't feel too much differently now. But I feel that I owe him, in some ways. For the man I am today, and for this tale. This all started because Angela needed help surprising him for their anniversary dinner, and nobody was able to distract the guy for a couple of hours while she set up. Well, what d'ya know? Big brother to the rescue.

I had sent him an awkward text message a few days earlier in a meager effort to appear as if I was planning an outing with him ahead of time. He normally didn't respond to my texts, and even though he answered this time, he immediately sensed that something was off.

I'm good, man. Is something wrong? What do you need?

Smug bastard. I swallowed my pride and let him know that I didn't need anything, that I was just interested in doing something after work on Thursday. Angela said I needed to stall him from six p.m. to eight p.m., the time during which he normally transported home, finished any outstanding work from the office, and started dinner for Angela. She would leave his first clue as to where to meet her for dinner at their house, so she couldn't have him there while she was setting the stage. I had a surprise for her, though. For both of them. She said she needed me to stall him, probably assuming we would go and get drinks or something. But I had something else in mind.

I walked out of the hotel at about 6:05 p.m. During the enterprise renovations last year, the company had opted to put the executive and presidential level offices as close to the flagship location in each priority market as possible. It worked well for me. I was able to relocate to the city Angela and I were raised in, instead of working at the corporate headquarters 1,100 miles away. I stepped into the transporter and scanned my I.D. and then my Gridlock card. Two minutes later, I was in the lobby of Gridlock, staring at the back of Daryl's head.

"Hey there, buddy. Sorry I'm a couple minutes late," I lied.

"It's no problem. Good to see you, man. How you been?" asked Daryl, cheerfully grinning, showing all of his teeth.

"Everything is everything. I see you're all dressed and ready."

"Yeah! I actually come here pretty often. I have a locker. I shot down a little early from work, so I could warm up and happened to see the manager on his way out. You know after five p.m., everything is automated. Great business model, saves them a ton of money. Anyway, I'm ready to go when you are. I'll be right here."

"Cool," I grumbled, and headed downstairs to get changed.

Daryl having a membership at Gridlock was the first unexpected wrinkle in my plan. He worked as the assistant athletic director at the university, and I knew that he had played baseball in college, but that was some time ago. I wanted to bring him there to embarrass him, so I tried to choose something physically daunting, because frankly, I wasn't sure I could outsmart or out-charm or even outdrink the guy. But I was pretty certain that I could out-athlete him. Right up until the point in time where I transported into the lobby of the training facility and saw him shadowboxing with the speed of Sugar Ray Leonard.

I finished lacing up my shoes and took a swig of my energy drink. I studied myself in the mirror and decided to do a few push-ups before I went back upstairs.

Gridlock is a high-intensity, physical training facility. No, no. It's more of an environment than a facility, that is to say, all of the structures are simulated. Digitally. But, unlike holograms, you can actually touch and feel them. If you can imagine a huge warehouse with a stark white, sterile interior, you're halfway there. Inside the warehouse are one main lobby and several rooms around the perimeter. The locker room and showers are downstairs. It's almost like playing in a virtual reality game, except you're really there. You enter one of the rooms, and the environment shifts, molds, and adjusts itself into a certain scenario, right before your eyes. The world's brightest graphic designers and engineers, the types of folks who invented 3-D printing, are credited with making Gridlock a success. The scenarios are all environments, unconventional places that allow you to get in a great workout. They're normally a creative twist on traditional workout locations. Maybe you end up on an Olympic track or maybe it's a boxing ring where the canvas rotates, who knows? New environments are always being designed. Gridlock was founded maybe five years ago as a result of some governmental technology being relinquished to the public domain. Almost all of the expenditures associated with running a Gridlock facility were investment costs and offshore maintenance and management, and the "sport" of franchising Gridlock locations was a gold mine for bigwigs who had a little extra money to spend. The lobby was circular and metallic. A tiny receptionist's desk sat in the left corner, and around the arc of what was the circular lobby were several doors.

Training rooms.

The rooms were situated by level. The higher the room number, the higher the level of proficiency needed to access the individual environment or "grid." Outside of each room was a panel that gave you the option among several grids unique to that room. These grids rotated based on season, special event, or sometimes just because a developer came up with something new. I motioned for Daryl to follow me over toward level six, the highest Gridlock level available.

"We going into level eight?" Daryl asked.

I probably seemed more naive than confused.

"No. Six," I said, impatiently tapping the placard right outside the door as I scanned my membership card and the door opened.

"Oh, my bad. I haven't done six in a while. It'll be refreshing," said Daryl, curtly.

At this point, my annoyance and confusion were about level. I had to ask.

"What do you mean? Six is as high as Gridlock goes...at this location," I quickly added as the thought came to me that maybe he had attended a more advanced Gridlock in some far off place.

"Nah, man," Daryl laughed. "So there's this whole secret world of Gridlock. Angela told me you come here a ton so I figured you knew all about all the extra stuff. It looks so neat and simple, but in reality, there are a bunch of hidden features. For example, the lost levels—seven and eight—can only be accessed through the entrance to level six. Here, look."

He was right. The doors opened, and he immediately located a tiny, dull light embedded in the right wall of the foyer of the level six environment. I had never noticed the light, but there were so many bells and whistles inside each environment, I was sure that even if I had seen it I would not have assumed it to be anything special.

"Tap your card twice on that light right there," said Daryl.

I tapped. Nothing happened.

"Hmm. You're not cleared. Crazy, they normally clear you for level seven and eight after you've completed enough grids in six. You do six a lot? Or did you just get up to this level?"

"I've done six *plenty* of times," I snapped. It was true. I had been exercising in level six for over a year. I wasn't sure why I didn't have access to the other levels, or why nobody had even told me that there were other levels. I was embarrassed and angry. My plan was backfiring, and we hadn't even started yet. Daryl tapped his card twice on the light, and it turned purple and began to swirl. A holographic keypad displayed on the wall, and Daryl spoke the code "092991." The wall split in the middle and revealed a room similar to the lobby. Cold, sterile. The only pathetic attempt at comfort was a white couch seated across from a water fountain in the middle of the room. The room was rectangular, and from the entrance where we stood, we could see two large steel doors on the other side of the room. Seven and eight.

"You want some water?"

With all of my plans for the night having failed thus far, I had become insecure and unconfident. I took offense to everything that Daryl asked, even if he meant well. Admittedly, that wasn't much different than how I normally related to him, but I was hypersensitive in this particular situation.

"I'm fine," I said, walking toward level eight.

"You want to start with seven? The difficulty is pretty much the same between seven and eight. I don't know. I just like to go in order, I guess. I'm weird like that. And I know you haven't done seven yet."

"Eight is fine; can you let us in?" I asked impatiently.

Daryl chuckled and scanned his card into level eight. Only one grid option presented itself, which was strange, to Daryl and me. For the first time that night, we were on the same page.

"Weird. Maybe the other ones are under maintenance or something. The cool thing about level eight is usually that they are a bunch of different enviros to choose from. Because it's the last level and all, you know? They try not to let you get bored. I've never done this grid before though. You up for it?"

"Go for it."

Daryl scanned into the grid called *Industrial Park*, and we stepped in. A muggy brown fog shrouded us as the door closed behind us and then dematerialized. There were no take-backs in Gridlock. Once you entered an environment, you had to complete the course. The managers could make an exit available in emergency situations, and after hours, the offshore technicians monitored each in-use facility in case of a calamity. Only those with athletic prowess and experience are encouraged to use Gridlock environments, and each facility member has to be Gridlock-certified before participating in any environment.

As the fog cleared, the first thing I noticed was that the grid was much vaster than any I had ever been in. Typically, they were built to be naturally conducive to a circuit workout. Although each grid within each level was relatively intensive, you usually began in the middle and could navigate your way around and around until your time limit or progress goals were completed. But not this time. The industrial park seemed linear, and the same muddy fog shrouded the better part of the environment off in the distance. We really could see only several yards in front of us. I could sense Daryl felt something was awry as well.

"I've never seen one like this."

I remained quiet. Of course he knew I hadn't either.

"It's weird; it must not be for circuit training like the others. And it's so foggy. Not sure I like this setup."

"Well, once we're in, we're in. Or is there some type of special, frequent-user privilege that lets you transport out of environments prematurely?" He didn't register my sarcasm, which made me feel dumb.

"No, no, you're right about that. We're here now. Might as well go for it. The first course is up there; let's go take a look."

We adjusted our clothes and breathing masks. There were special masks available for use while in Gridlock that helped to regulate breathing. They were designed for use in high-altitude environments so that athletes could train without fear of passing out. But more experienced Gridlockers like myself, and Daryl as well, liked to use them in all new grids as a way to develop muscle memory of managing our energy while completing courses. I strapped mine on tight and proceeded through the smog alongside Daryl. After a couple of minutes, our first course came completely into view. I had never seen anything like it.

Ahead of us was a football-field-length plot, organized into long columns, like a vertical garden. Each column stretched the entire length of the field, and I might mention that we weren't quite sure where the field ended because the smog picked up at the end of the visible portion of the course. Every column was moving, horizontally. The lines themselves slowly slid across the width of the plot, one replacing the other's previous position in a continuous flow. As we stepped right up to the start of the course, we noticed that the columns were wide enough for two people.

"Guess we're running together," Daryl smirked.

Then, I noticed the most crucial aspect of the course.

Each column was filled with sand. The dozens of columns shifting horizontally were each filled with it, thousands and thousands of grains tumbling over and over each other as the entire plot of the field shifted beneath them. Gridlock is new-worldly, intensive athletic training. I've bouldered in an Alps environment. Plate-pushed in a sauna. Box-jumped in a hyper-gravity room. I had never seen anything as daunting as that sand field. Suddenly, something protruded from under the first column of sand. It was a rectangular plastic box, empty save for a tiny laminated card taped to the base of the container.

Shoes

We removed our shoes and stepped onto the platform. It took a few seconds to synchronize our watches. I heard the familiar Gridlock horns that signified the start of a course. Then there was Mona, the omnipresent personification of Gridlock. Her sweet monotone filled the environment, and I let all my inhibitions go. I was in the zone.

3...2...1

The horns blared, and Daryl blazed off ahead of me. He was the fastest person I had ever seen with my own two eyes. He was quickly and easily ten yards ahead of me before I had time to catch my stride. I figured he was a pitcher in college from his build, but he may have been a pinch runner. I was so focused on Daryl, I almost failed to adjust my steps to shift me into my new lane as my column shifted to the right. As soon as my feet hit the sand in the second column, I lost all faith in my ability to complete the course. I was only about twenty-five yards down the never-ending field, and my legs were on fire. Daryl was about forty yards ahead of me with no signs of slowing. But it was specifically the way my foot hit the sand in the second column that clued me into the futility of my run. My first step was a sinking one, right into a deep trough. It took a hell of a spring off my left leg to propel me out of the rut, so I could continue running. I tried to stay light on my feet for the second step, but I sank again. I may not have been as strong as Daryl, but I'm no dummy.

Each column had a different type of sand in it. If this entire course was a desert biome, then the columns were Saharan, Sonoran, and Gobi in nature. A column of dry, tight sand was followed by a loose sinking spread, which was succeeded by sprawling waves with high dunes. I nearly needed to jump over them to continue moving forward. I wasn't athletic enough to compete in this environment. The speed of the horizontal shift was increasing the farther downfield we ran, and the sand in each column was so vastly different, it was almost impossible for me to adjust in time. I focused all my energy on remaining upright, not falling. My pace slowed considerably as I heaved my way downfield. After a while, I could see Daryl stopped in the distance.

I was annoyed at having lost the first course but elated that the field indeed ended at the re-introduction of brown smog.

I jogged to a stop and tried to regulate my breathing, so I wouldn't look too pitiful. Daryl tossed me a bottle of water and my sneakers as I finished running. I drank thirstily and almost choked on the water. I coughed several times, and Daryl patted my back. I moved beyond his reach to finish my coughing in peace. I took a few more sips, slowly, and turned to face Daryl and the smog.

"Level eight, huh?"

"Man," Daryl's face twisted in a show of genuine perplexity. "I've never run a grid like this. It was extremely difficult. Even in relation to the other level eights I've done. My legs are killing me."

I took a couple more sips as I finished lacing my shoes. I felt a bit redeemed. He had thought it was difficult too, which meant I wasn't as talentless as I had feared.

"What did you play anyway? Shortstop? First base, probably, huh?"

"What?" Daryl asked, confused.

"Angela said you played baseball at the university. You're pretty damn fast; what position did you play?"

"Did she say that? Ha, that woman, man. Sometimes she's loopy. I ran track. I was a sprinter, and I did some relays too, in my last year."

"Oh. That explains that, then."

Shit! I hate being embarrassed. And this was the umpteenth time that day. Of course he had run track. Angela *met* him at the track. She was an athletic trainer at the school for a couple years before going back for her degree in physical therapy. She didn't meet him until his last year, which was strange because she had been a trainer the entire year before that. I have no clue where I got baseball from, but it was clear that I either cared nothing about him or I didn't listen to my sister, both of which were true enough. And of course, ever-pleasant Daryl absorbed my ignorant mistake and blamed it on my sister in the name of "guy-code." He'd probably go home and talk all types of shit about how I was being intentionally petty toward him. Or even worse, he wouldn't.

"I figure we'll be here for a while, just because I expect the courses to get harder. You about ready for the next one?" he asked.

"Sure, let's go."

I tried to stand up, and my legs buckled. Daryl noticed and tried to suppress a brief chuckle. We walked through the brown smog, and the environment instantly grew much darker. A chill accompanied the darkness and swept across our bodies in brisk breezes. The farther we walked, the darker it became until neither one of us could see in front of us. I continued walking, hands outstretched, figuring eventually we'd run into something, a light would come on, or the horns would blare. There was no need for paranoia in Gridlock, no need for precaution. Everything went as planned. In the rare case that an answer wasn't easily discernable, it would be revealed in due time. Faith in the system was a major aspect of enjoying the Gridlock experience. Sure, the grids were potentially dangerous, but the bottom line was that people went there to work out. What harm could the managers of such a facility seek to bring to us? Athletes, patrons, meatheads. You go with the flow. You put one foot ahead of the other. At least, that's how I felt, before Daryl fell.

As soon as the moonlight peeked in through the top of the grid, any shadow of concern that we had vanished. We could see well enough to know that we were walking on some sort of grassy plateau. I had noticed we were in an elevated environment while stepping through the dark; my mask had helped adjust my breathing to the altitude. We had enough moonlight to see each other and the area in which we stood. I could see my breath wisp through the night air. Before I knew it, Daryl was slipping, screaming, and falling off the edge of the plateau. I screamed out to him, but he was already out of sight. I rushed to the spot where he had fallen. The Gridlock horns blared in the background as Mona counted down. I lost whatever screams Daryl emitted in the cacophony of the surrounding noise mixed with my own terrified thoughts.

Mona was finished counting, and I was supposed to be starting the course, but I didn't know what to do. I peered over the edge of the plateau and saw that it was a long way down and at the bottom of the canyon was a rushing river. I took my mask off and breathed deeply. The air was sharp and tight in my lungs—I hadn't fully adjusted to the altitude yet. I took off my shoes again, zipped my jacket up to my chin, closed my eyes, and leapt off of the plateau.

I tried to hold my breath until I hit the water, but I had underestimated how far down I would have to fall before reaching the bottom of the chasm. About halfway down, my lungs about to burst, I begin flailing and gasping for air. I never understood why gasping and flailing were directly proportional. I tried to suck in big gulps, but the air rushed up from under me so fast, it seemed like all the air I was struggling to breathe in was climbing over me and pushing me down. I plummeted into the stream, which thankfully turned out to be more of a lake. The flailing and gasping continued until I swam upward and broke the surface of the water, eventually paddling over and resting on a slippery rock. I noticed that the stream pooled at the waterfall, which meant that technically our course had started at "the end." I would have to swim against the current, the only direction that led anywhere, in order to progress. I pushed off the rock and began to swim. It had been a while since I had done a pool workout. They were my favorite in college. I quickly adjusted to the waves, like riding a bike, but I kept in mind that swimming was much more tiring than it appeared, and I knew that not having utilized certain muscles in years combined with having tortured my legs in the sand field meant that I could only swim for so long.

The stream narrowed as it flowed through a cavernous structure. I stood up where the water became shallow and walked through the cave. It was quiet. The peace was unnerving. I had never been in a grid that was quiet; the raucous environmental noises mixed with the grunts and hollers of athletes normally made the soundtrack for a grid. The quiet cave seemed sinister. And then it began to spin.

The entire cave began to roll, like a giant hamster wheel. The shallow water splashed around, building a tiny wave as the cavern walls began to spin faster. I bolted to the right side of the cave and began to run. I had to run diagonally on the cavern wall to avoid falling into the water as the hamster wheel turned. But the walls of the cavern were moist and slippery, and I fell into the water twice. As I quickly rose to run again after the second fall, I heard the crashing of a wave. I turned from where I had come to see the entire mouth of the cave filled with water. The next wave was nearly fifty feet tall, and set to break right on top of me. I would drown in the cave before I could ever swim my way out. I took off once again toward the exit of the cave, which was now in my sight. I could feel the wave creeping toward me, hovering over me, whispering *futility* onto my neck with frozen breath. I ran until I was submerged in fear and icy tide. And once submerged I swam. The deluge spit me out at the exit of the cave onto a dry sandy shore. I coughed most of the water out of my lungs and examined the shore. It was about four feet by four feet with one tall vertical pole sprouting from its center. I looked up to the top of the pole and noticed that it was swaying to and fro. The top of the pole was situated between two tall plateaus like the one on which we had begun. During one of the sways toward the plateau to the left of me, I saw a figure fly off the pole onto the grassy highland. I wiped the water from my eyes and watched the figure stand, wipe himself off, and wave down to me, shouting something inaudible.

Daryl.

"You've got to climb!" he screamed.

The pole was at least thirty feet tall. I squinted up toward where he was and started to think maybe life wasn't so bad on my four-foot-by-four-foot plot. I could probably get used to it, if I tried.

***

I had zero energy left after flinging myself onto the mesa where Daryl waited. I had almost slipped amidst all the swaying, and although I'm sure I could have died, in the moment I didn't fear for my life. Nobody ever died in a grid. The thought was almost ridiculous. I'd never been first at anything in my life, so I had pretty low confidence about being the first guy to die in Gridlock. Still, Daryl seemed concerned, and the part of me that accepted his prowess in the environment as superior to mine shared his concern.

"Something isn't right."

I sat on the mesa with an aerial view of the lands surrounding the plateau. It looked as if we had made a complete circle since the moon first illuminated our whereabouts.

"I think something is wrong with this level. I've never seen this grid listed before; I've never seen courses like this...it just feels...off."

"I've never been in a grid with a glitch in it," I admitted, "but it seems like if anything had gone unplanned up until now, offshore technical support would have already intervened. Maybe you just slipped. It happens."

"Happens all the time. But never at the start of a course. Most courses, the first step you need to take to begin the course isn't even accessible until after the countdown. I fell off the plateau before Mona even started counting."

"But you also said this grid is unlike any you've ever done before, so how do we know that's not normal? We were confused and unsuspecting. It was scary for a moment, but it doesn't really seem like there's anything fundamentally flawed with the grid. Just a stroke of bad luck."

Daryl pondered my comments for a moment and nodded his head. "Maybe you're right. It's been a long day; I'm probably just tired and not as sharp as I should be. How long have we been in here anyway?"

I looked down at my watch and noticed that the face was blank. Washed out from the water for sure. Of course, Daryl's watch was inoperative too. There were no clocks in the grid, so not only did we not have a clue how long we'd been there, we didn't know what time it was either.

"Shit, I'm supposed to be getting you to dinner; we have to get out of here."

"To where?"

I froze. Damn! I had let the secret slip. I had almost forgotten the only reason we were here was to stall long enough to allow Angela to set the stage for the evening. I hoped he wouldn't pay any attention to what I said. We would hurry up and finish the grid, and I would get him home. I would play it cool about the dinner and be really vague. He would have no idea what I was talking about.

"So, Angela is using you to stall me for some anniversary thing she's planning, huh?"

He knew exactly what I was talking about.

"Ha. That makes perfect sense. I felt like it was pretty weird when you reached out, honestly. I know we don't hang like that. Angela was really pressing it too, almost like I'd be doing you a favor by hanging out. Jeez. She's a good gal, Angela is. But this. This is too much, man. We shouldn't be going through all this just because you needed to kill some time. We could have hit a bar. I say we get out of here. Promise I'll pretend like I'm still surprised."

My heart was in my throat. I was failing at every aspect of this entire evening, and now I had ruined Angela's surprise for Daryl. I could barely cough my words out. I sputtered out some unintelligible mumbles as my voice cracked, and I struggled to recoup from my blunder.

"Uh...get out, what do you mean? You have to complete a grid to be granted exit access, right?"

"Not with level eight clearance."

"I should have known."

"Yeah, we just have to find the next course. I'll scan my card at the start, we'll be transported back to the locker rooms and have the option to restart at our checkpoint if we ever come into this grid again."

"Well, I mean, it can't be that much longer until we finish. Even though it's been fewer courses than usual, they've taken considerably longer to complete than normal. We probably only have one more. In which case, I think we might as well complete it."

"I don't know, man. I'm kind of tired."

"I'm not," I lied.

"Ha. Well sure. I get a layout of all the remaining courses in this grid once I scan my card at the start of the next one. We'll see how many we have left and go from there."

I wasn't sure why I wanted to win. I didn't care about the courses or the environment itself. I didn't want to finish the grid, and I could barely walk, let alone compete in anything else athletic, especially against Daryl. But I didn't want him to be *right*. I never had, and I don't think I ever will. I had within my grasp the only semblance of a time where my decision-making could be heralded over his. He had come into my sister's life and made me completely obsolete. I was never the best brother to her growing up. How good can a teenage brother really be? She had found someone who was nearly perfect, and as the only other man who had ever been a part of her life, I was always in juxtaposition to him. I was fine being insecure in my own shitty bubble of a world. But having my flaws and shortcomings on continuous display anytime Daryl was around or spoken about was just too much for me. I hated looking at him and hated listening to him because it always reminded me that I could never be him. I had never envied another human before, but I would have given anything to be like the one my sister married. Yet, I knew I couldn't, and the frustration and resentment that bubbled out of that cauldron of covetousness was like venom in my veins. I was itching to sink my fangs into him on the unlikely occasion that the opportunity presented itself.

We stood, and the grid went dark again, but this time, the lights flickered rapidly before a blinding wave of illumination bathed us. As the luminance declined, my vision strengthened. The grid got darker and darker until reaching the ambience of a photo development room, a warm, reddish light barely making visible a great wall which stood before us.

At first I thought that it was a rock-climbing wall, because spread out across the black marble material were myriad colored stones in a seemingly random assortment. It really did look like a huge, black rock-climbing wall, but I knew there had to be something more to it. I just didn't know what. The wall was wide, with deep fluorescent cracks running all through it. I had trouble distinguishing where the black of the wall began from where it blended into the shadowy grid environment. It would be like climbing the night sky.

"Stadiums," Daryl called out.

"Huh?"

"Stadiums. We're supposed to run stadiums up and down this wall."

"How the hell are we supposed to do that? There's 100 percent incline."

"Looks like that's the point. You see these cracks? They're bifurcations. They separate each set of 'steps' from the next. These stones look random, but there is a certain path of them that will take us straight up the wall. We run up this side here," he said, pointing to the left, "make a lateral move to the right, and then run down this side here. The end of the wall is to the right over there somewhere. We can't see it, but I assume that as we progress to the right, the grid will illuminate it for us."

"You going to scan your card?"

"What? Oh! Man, I almost forgot. Well, you said you wanted to stay and finish right? I'm doubtful there could be many more grids."

"Why don't we just scan and see?"

"Sure, thing."

Daryl scanned his card at the leftmost corner of the wall. A hologram map of the grid reflected before our very eyes. We saw that there were only two more courses in the grid. One was the wall that we currently faced, and although we could tell that there was another, it was obscured on the hologram. We couldn't tell what the course challenge would be. The hologram disappeared, and Daryl turned to face me.

"Only one more course after this one. You ready to knock this out?"

Arrogant Daryl. Omnipotent Daryl. He always knew everything. It was my idea to stay and complete the grid, but as he assessed the difficulty and found the solution, he became more energized than ever about climbing the wall. I had noticed the glee in his eyes as he explained how to move up and down the stadium wall. How quickly he had forgotten about his distrust of the system. How insignificant his fatigue as he salivated over the opportunity to solve another problem, to be a hero yet again. Had he no integrity? He was a man trapped by his own obsessive compulsion. How weak. He couldn't even attend to his physiological needs in the face of nourishment that might feed a greater hunger. His ego was ravenous enough to consume even himself. He had everyone else fooled with the "nice, sensible guy" gag, but I knew the truth.

"Let's go for it," I said.

Daryl and I took our places at the base of the wall. I was still shoeless, but I wasn't concerned. It would all be over soon. I heard Mona's smooth tenor fill the environment yet again. She counted down, and the all too familiar horns blared.

3...2...1

Daryl jetted upward on the steep wall. Each step was the size and shape of a rock on a climbing wall, and the wall was completely vertical. There was no way he'd make it to the top and back down. Gravity would stop him long before he achieved any type of success. Fool. My legs were heavy and weak. I jogged up a few of the steps and waited. I looked up to see Daryl very near the top of the wall where he would have to make a horizontal move to start his ascent down the second section of the wall. It was almost time.

As Daryl made the lateral move, I hopped the short distance down from the wall and stepped back. The wall began to rumble and quake, the sound of thunder emitting from the cracks in the wall as they transformed into fissures. I heard Daryl's familiar scream approaching from the top of the wall, echoing through the night. Closer, closer, closer…

His body crumpled pathetically as it hit the ground. I stared into his eyes as the last life drained from them, the dim red light catching the last twinkle of his glassy gaze. He coughed and sputtered, undoubtedly trying to squeak out some famous last words. "*Et tu, Brute?*" or some shit like that. I refused to let them be heard. I walked to the left of the wall and noticed that it had shaken loose from the precipice onto which it was mounted. One of the poles the team had used to mount the black marble wall jutted out, sharp and stark against the darkness of the grid. Which reminded me.

"You guys can bring the lights up."

At once the entire grid was bright, and the wall receded until it was out of my sight. The mesas, off in the distance, flattened and the water rushed out of the chasm and into nothingness. The entire surface of the grid leveled out, and a plain white world remained where chaos had once reigned. I had almost forgotten about Daryl's body. I walked over to it and saw that he was already dead; he had spent his last moments alone, with no one to cry to, no one to mourn him. Exactly how I wanted it.

"Is there anything else we can do for you, sir?"

The offshore rep had patched into the environment's sound system to communicate with me.

"Get rid of this," I poked Daryl's body with my foot. "And delete this grid. Good work on it. For what we needed it for, of course. Don't ever make anything this fucking hard for training purposes."

"Yes, of course, sir."

A couple of blinks later, I had been transported to the locker room.

***

I undressed and jumped in the shower. The story was simple. Daryl had never showed up to Gridlock. I had scheduled my assistant to place two calls to Angela from my office phone, one at 6:48 p.m. and another at 7:03 p.m. These were the times I had calculated that she would be most busy setting up and likely would not answer. Although I had told Daryl to meet me at Gridlock, she believed that I had changed the plans the day of and asked him to meet me at the office. Those missed calls would make it look like I had tried to call her when I couldn't locate Daryl, and then proceeded on to Gridlock when I couldn't reach her. She wouldn't have been able to return my calls because I was gone from the office and my cellphone was "dead."

The narrative that I had never seen Daryl that day would keep me from having to explain any aspect of what happened to him. The less I had to do of that, the better. There would be a missing persons case and a search, but they would never find him. I had enlisted the help of my top designer in creating the *Industrial Park* Gridlock experience, as well as paying him a hefty bonus to ensure that the entire grid was wiped clean and never utilized ever again. You see, I had been the franchiser of this Gridlock location since its origin. Years and years in executive positions in the hospitality industry had made me a ton of money, which I saved mostly and reinvested sparingly.

As I mentioned before, when architects first came to the city presenting about Gridlock, it was much too sweet of an opportunity to pass up if you had any money. You'd recoup initial investment costs within the first five years, and operating costs were so minimal in relation to scale that upkeep was nearly non-existent. The offshore labor was cheap, and the workers were diligent. I had jumped at the chance to franchise a Gridlock location, and once I won the bid, I negotiated to have my location be the only one in a 50-mile radius. Afterward, I made sure I had the best designers and the most sleek, modern appearance for my location. It was the most popular thing in town. I could live the rest of my life off the profits of this Gridlock location alone.

The shower was cold, which helped keep me alert. I really was tired, but I knew there was a long night of dramatics ahead. The sooner the whirlwind began, the sooner it could end. I practiced my surprised and empathetic faces in the mirror. I had another audition for best big brother, and I would be sure to win the part this time. After I was dressed, I walked out of the locker room and killed the lights in every room I passed through until I got to the exit of the building. I punched in the security code to the complex. Gridlock normally stayed open all hours, but this was a holiday weekend. Staying away from the building would help keep me in the holiday spirit.

The Town of Our Lady

Queen of the Angels...

C all me crazy. Go ahead, I know you will. I swear, I have angels looking out for me. And dude, I know everybody says that like, all the time, but man, I'm like, so serious. Like, as far back as I can remember, they've been coming down with their little wings and pullin' me outta shit. Well, not literally you know, but they've been there! Disguised as people and things you would never even think to pay attention to.

And man, have I been in some shit. Let me tell you.

Like that time when I was twelve, and Tommy Nelson and his cousin chased me down my block after school for talking smack to them earlier that morning. Tommy was none too bright, but he was one of those big suckers. You know, one of those supposed-to-be ninth-graders who "mysteriously" found himself still in the sixth grade year after year...after year? Well, I swear the kid ran an NFL combine-worthy time down the block because I had a twenty-yard head start when we got off the bus, but that didn't last any longer than Tommy's hopes of getting promoted to a higher grade at the end of each semester. I could feel his hot breath on my neck. My legs got heavy. It felt like I was swimming instead of running. He pulled me by the back of my collar, and I let my body go limp, trying to get ready for the impact I knew I was coming but feared all the same.

Much to my surprise, I didn't find myself in Tommy's clutches after he yanked me up and I played possum in midair. I hit the asphalt hard. All the breath shot out of my chest like a bottle rocket. I heard footsteps trailing off in the opposite direction. I turned and watched Tommy and his cousin running for their lives from some huge dog. Pit bull, might have been. Now I know this doesn't sound so crazy. But there were no pit bulls on my block. *Man, nobody even owned dogs on my street.* Oh, go ahead! Say he was a stray, I know you will. But the fact of the matter is…that pit bull…was an angel. Yes, dogs can be angels too. They all go to Heaven, duh.

But anyway, back to my point. I know angels are real, man. And they're all around us. I figure it's kinda like what they say about magic, you know? If you don't believe, then you can't ever really notice it. Well, I believe all right.

I worked at my internship only on Monday and Tuesday, so every other morning, I'd run a few miles around the neighborhood. Or bike more than a few. Just depended on how I felt. Down La Brea, back up North Gardner, or maybe North Highland if I was feeling adventurous. I normally tried to avoid central Hollywood. Buncha weirdos, man. I had shipped out to Los Angeles without much notice from my sweet home Alabama. Everybody likes to think we're none too bright down home, but that's only half true. We got about the same amount of smartie-Arties and fall-behind Freds as any other place, I reckon. Anyhow, I had gotten an internship with PlaneSocial, a tech startup that was trying to revolutionize app development at the time, specifically for news outlet-sharing through social media. I missed Alabama a ton, but I hadn't left much behind. I told Ma I'd be gone for the summer, packed a bag, got some cash from my savings, and headed out.

But I had applied for this internship much earlier and never heard back. Everybody at the company did so many different jobs, the developer/content manager/internship program coordinator/lunch-grabber-for-everybody-because-i'm-the-new-guy-even-though-the-company-is-only-five-years-old had forgotten that he had to do the internship coordinator part.

Better than forgetting the lunch-grabber part, for his sake.

So my application had gotten lost under a stack of briefings and stale pizza crusts. But when the spring bloomed, and the office manager/payroll administrator/parking validator/lead accountant remembered that you could write interns off on your taxes if you paid them for at least twenty hours a week and filed with a certain status, they finally threw away those pizza crusts and called in the big guns. It was pretty rude of them, if you ask me. They were lucky I didn't have something better to do. Just kidding. Sort of.

But anyway, back to my point. I did my morning jog and circled right back around to the condo I was staying in. I had moved to L.A. without really knowing anybody or having anywhere to stay. I was planning to get a room at an extended stay and ride it out until I joined the Terracotta Army of the homeless out there, but I posted an ad (more like a beggar's soliloquy) on my Facebook before I boarded the plane saying if anybody knew anybody who knew anybody in L.A. who would be willing to put me up for the first part of the summer, then I'd surely split my internship money with them (the value is all in the experience!) and would stay out of their way as much as possible. I got plenty of hits on the post congratulating me and asking what I'd be doing, but only one relevant reply.

Shelly-Ann Thomas messaged me saying that her grandma lived just west of Hollywood, even closer to my internship than I was originally planning on staying. She explained that her folks were originally from out there. It made sense; Shelly-Ann was a weirdo. She said her grandma lived in a one-bedroom condo in a quiet complex and that she was super-nice. She was sure if I agreed to clean up after myself and not have guests over, then she would allow me to stay there. The woman loved Shelly-Ann and would do anything for her friends. Shelly-Ann and I weren't friends; she was a weirdo. But, hey, that seemed to be what would oil the old lady's hinges, so I went with it. Shelly-Ann put in the good word for me and boom, $150 a month to stay in the living room of a condo in L.A. on a pullout couch.

One day, I came back to the complex after a run. Grandma Greasy Hinges lived in the back of the complex, so I had to walk down a long path before I could shower and put my feet up. The walk wasn't bad though. Summer is pretty in Los Angeles. A ton of flowers: blues, pinks, purples dancing in the light breeze. Every day was around eighty degrees. Never too hot or too cold. And it never rained, not one time the whole summer. Well, I was walking on this path when I saw him. Or he saw me I guess. I don't remember. There were a ton of people who lived in the complex who I didn't know, so it would never have struck me that I didn't recognize him. Anyway, it's like he was nowhere, and then he was right there. He was standing in front of me so close that I probably couldn't have taken another step without walking all over him. But he wasn't blocking my path in an invasive way. He was turned to the side, discarding weeds he had pulled from around some shrubs. He looked at me with a serious grin. I don't know if that makes sense. A serious grin. He looked like he knew something I didn't. Something important. But it wasn't a boastful look. It was almost like he knew I'd know what he knew, eventually. He was confident in it. But for the meantime, I had no idea who the hell this wiry black man was and why he was grinning at me. I just assumed he was a weirdo.

"How was your run? What's your name?" he asked, extending his hand.

"Pretty good, uh…thanks. I'm Davis. Nice day out, eh? I see you tending to your flowers."

"Their splendor is all their own. Football, your sport of choice, huh? Big in the south I know. Your accent would say 'Bama, maybe?

He had seen the football emblem on my workout shirt from high school. I wasn't aware that I had any kinda accent, but I mean some people have an ear for that kinda thing. Seems like football was the main, if not only thing folks from outside of Alabama knew about Alabama. I grew tired of answering questions about it, mainly because I hated clichés, but also because my high school team was nowhere near as good as the famous ones.

"Yep, 'Bama is right."

"Thought so.

There was a brief pause. The man cocked his head with a curious smile.

"Has anyone ever told you...that you look very much like your father?"

I froze. I didn't know my father. He had been a big football star in our hometown twenty years ago or so. Unfortunately, that's where he peaked. He got my mother pregnant, didn't get into college, and just kinda faded away. People didn't chase things in my town. Folks mostly lived like leaves in the wind, drifting here and there, making the best out of wherever they got blown. My whole life, people from around the town told me I was the spitting image of my pop. It meant nothing to me. What's the spitting image of a ghost anyway? Just a reminder of somebody who hurt you when they left. But where was I? Oh yeah.

"I...I...huh?" I stammered.

"Your father. Your face, your features tell me they were passed down from your dad. I wouldn't be surprised if you two looked like twins."

"I've never met him," he added. "Just a feeling I had."

"Yeah? Well, me neither."

"Maybe one day," he said consolingly. "Davis, you seem like a good kid. You're intelligent, driven. It seems like you have a plan. And you're aware. Self-aware mostly, which is incredibly important. I know you will do good things. I know you will be successful."

"Uh, thanks...I—,"

He smiled and placed his hand on my shoulder like the principal does when you win the spelling bee.

"Enjoy this California weather, Davis."

And just as suddenly as he had appeared, he disappeared. I honestly couldn't even tell you which apartment he went into.

That night, I thought about everything the man had told me. There really had never been anybody who had said the things he had said to me. I wasn't from an inspirational, supportive town. You either left and got forgotten, or stayed and became one of the zombies: mindless folks doing mindless jobs—shells of their former selves, once enlivened by hopes and dreams. Honestly, the main thing that had motivated me to do well was everybody around me expecting nothing more than mediocrity. I guess I always had a chip on my shoulder. I always thought of myself as a jet, using the apathy as fuel that would propel me to the moon. But the conversation earlier that day had made me feel like a flower. His words were the sunlight, strengthening and empowering me to reach new heights. I went to bed at peace and woke up determined.

I did really well at PlaneSocial over the next month or so. Even though I only got paid for twenty hours a week, most weeks I'd go in a couple extra days and help out around the office, or else I'd shadow one of the programmers and try to pick up some new skills. I ended up coding a fix to a really tricky bug in their newest application. The team there was about as excited as a group of tech nerds can be, and they even bought me a nice lunch as a bonus. I felt unstoppable. Limitless, you could say, like in that movie. I became well-known among some of the business partners around the office, and the PlaneSocial team even gave me responsibilities outside of typical "intern duties."

Life was beautiful. I enjoyed the L.A. sun and paid Grandma Greasy Hinges in all cash. I made a photo album of my experiences that summer. I captured pictures of the flowers—all the various colors in all their splendor. I even hung out with the other interns on the weekends sometimes. I had almost forgotten about the man.

But that wouldn't make for much of a story, now would it?

It was a clear Friday afternoon, the wind a little cooler than usual. I sat cross-legged on an enormous green lawn in the middle of Grandma Greasy Hinges' community. There was a really pretty stone fountain in the middle of the green, and the running water was relaxing. I was never too keen on poetry, but I'd sit out there and jot down a few lines of silly rhymes, maybe even write a letter to an old girlfriend that she'd never get to read. I remember days like this better than anything else. Although I didn't do much, I feel like those are the days that helped me grow the most. The introspection, the peace of mind, the calm—all these things worked together like the winds that push the clouds away from the sun. They helped me see what was really important—to understand it, to bathe in it, to fall so in love with the idea of unlocking my potential that it was impossible for me not to chase my dreams .

But anyway, back to my point. I looked up and saw him circling the fountain. The same man from before. He wore a white T-shirt and linen pants. On his feet were the kind of sandals your old uncles wear at the family cookouts. His hair was sparse, short bristles. He waltzed around the fountain like he was stepping on velvet. In an almost trance-like dance, he lightly ran his fingers through the water as he circled the stone. I didn't think he noticed me approaching him until he spoke.

"Beautiful day, isn't it Davis?"

"Sure is," I said, trying to play it cool after having been caught creeping up on the guy. I know I looked like such a weirdo.

"How have things been?"

"Good. Really good, actually. I'm doing well at my internship, enjoying days like today. I feel great."

"Nothing like peace, huh?" he chuckled. "Most people I meet don't really understand the value of peace. It's so easy to cling to the parts of the world surrounding us. That attachment really isn't healthy, though. You start to love the wrong things; you have separation anxiety for possessions, perceptions, even people sometimes. There is very little good here, enough to fit in the palm of your hand. Now, *that* is easy enough to cling to. But most people...can't see the forest for the trees, to use a turn of phrase."

He smiled.

It was a phrase my grandmother had used my whole life, and probably for most of hers. It's when you look right at something but can't see what you're looking for because your vision ain't focused right. She would ask me to grab the vanilla extract out of the cabinet to put into the sweet potato pie mix. I would tear that cabinet apart, I swear, and then tell her "I can't find it, Ma." She'd come right over and grab it right off the front row. She couldn't fool me though; I knew she kept it hidden in her sleeve like those old magicians. She'd tip a little vanilla extract into the bowl and shake her head. *Boy, you can't see the forest for the trees.* She said it when I got a football scholarship to a private high school, and I had a hard time deciding between accepting it or staying with friends at our district high school. She said it when I complained about not having a date to senior prom after Jane Willoughby asked me to take her like 30,000 times. The last time she said it, I sat crying beside her hospital bed in her last few hours. Her hands got colder and colder. I hugged her and sobbed into her pillow. *I don't want you to go, Ma.* She used the little strength she had to stroke the back of my head and smirk like we were back in the kitchen baking pies. *Boy, you still can't see the forest for the trees can you?* I couldn't tell whether I was laughing or crying. She passed on a couple hours later. I miss my grandma.

I agreed with the man about clinging to worldly things. I wasn't Buddha or nothing—I enjoyed the hedonism entrenched in a good ice cream cone as much as the next big kid. But growing up, I never really had much to cling to, so I never really clung to much. The conversation was interesting. He was telling me how he had a big family, mostly brothers and uncles and cousins. Non-profit and volunteer work was somewhat of a family business. He said a bunch of them used to live in L.A. but had started leaving about ten years ago in droves. Said it was overrated.

"People don't want help, Davis; they just want acceptance. This city has a culture of freedom—which isn't a bad thing necessarily. But the way it's expressed worries me sometimes. People don't care what you do just as long as you don't monitor what they do too closely. You could be a murderer or a mailman. Most people won't double take when you walk by because they know at some point during their lives they had considered being both. It's liberating in a way, I understand. But I've seen that it allows for an abundance of people in this area to live lives that aren't really theirs. Everybody here is projecting, pretending...it's a costume party nightmare where the scariest thing in the world is for someone to take off your mask before you get theirs."

I had no clue what to say.

"Yeah...sometimes I wonder, like...what would happen if we could just start the world over, you know?"

I had no clue what had made me say that, especially since I had never actually wondered that before.

"I kinda feel like it's hard for good people, you know? You go out of your way to help somebody, or go the extra mile, and folks just want to take advantage. It's like you try to do good, and they want to get rid of you. Like being a good person negatively affects them directly," I said.

He turned his head to me slowly and studied me for a second. It felt like an eternity.

"Some people don't want us here, Davis. People like us. They try as hard as they can to get us out of the picture, just so they don't have to feel bad about themselves. Unfortunately, they often succeed. The whole 'power in numbers' bit. But it's all temporary. And it's all preparing us for a glorious life. It's coming soon. A much more glorious life than we live now. We'll just 'start the world over' and let the good guys run it...I'm glad you're doing well, Davis. Don't get too comfortable here, though. Don't let this place change you."

He chuckled and gave me his signature shoulder grab. We said our good-byes, and he walked away from the green toward the road. It seemed strange because no apartments were over there, and it was getting late. I figured maybe his car was parked over that way. I looked up and saw the first stars of the evening blinking in the summer sky.

The last time I saw him was the night before I left L.A. for good. I was a little tipsy walking home from one of the bars on the street adjacent to Grandma Greasy Hinges' community. I was emotional. My internship had ended the day before, and some of the interns and I had decided to have one last night at the bar before we parted ways for the school year. I didn't even drink usually. Like I said, I was emotional. I wasn't a city slicker by any means, but the world beyond 'Bama had given me a slice of life I'd never had. I was going to miss certain parts of it. The fear of becoming a neighborhood zombie was greater than ever before. I had seven months to figure out how to keep climbing. I was spoiled rotten. And I was emotional.

At first, I couldn't distinguish the flashing red and blue lights in the distance from the stars I was seeing with a drunken, hazy gaze. As I came closer, though, the unmistakable specter of a cop car revealed itself. I walked past the car and into the community garden. I was almost completely past the vehicle when I heard a muffled cough. I turned to see the man, leaning head-first out of the backseat of the squad car. His body hung limp, the back of his hand gently scraping the pavement as he lay nearly motionless. His eyes were closed, his mouth bloody. I could tell he was injured. My body went ice cold as I approached the car.

"Hey...hey!"

As soon as the officers saw me drawing nearer, they rushed to the side of the car I was on, yelling and screaming.

"Get back! What are you doing?! Back up!"

"Is he okay? Hey, man. Are you okay?"

"Shut up!"

"Y'all hurt him, man. He needs help! What's going on!?"

One of the officers walked towards me. He was a big man. It was night time, but when he stood over me I got even colder, like he had cast a shadow on me.

"Listen up, Son. We're about to take this guy in. Everything's fine, just keep heading to where you were going."

"But what happened?" I asked. Peering around the shoulder of Officer Shadow, I noticed that the other cop had stood the man up and leaned him against the squad car. His body was still slack as the officer turned him around to cuff him.

"This guy and guys like him have been causing trouble around here for years. We're cracking down on them. We've almost dissipated the group down to a few core members. We won't have to wo—

"Davis…"

The voice was weak and raspy. I barely heard it beneath Shadow's voice. I slid past him quickly and ran to the man. The closer I got, the more concerned I was. His face was beaten badly. His eyes were swollen nearly shut. A trickle of blood climbed down carefully from his lip to his chin.

"What did they do!!!!???" I screamed. I started to cry. The fear was like venom in my veins. I felt my world slowing down. Everyone was yelling, and Shadow was pulling me away from the man. I hung on to him as hard as I could, for no real reason I guess. Then he said it again.

"Davis…"

"Yes?" I muttered through teary eyes, pulling with all my weight against Shadow's grasp.

He reached his hand out and for only a split second, between Shadow's and my tug of war, grazed my shoulder.

"Start over."

I don't know what happened after that. I lost all my energy. I couldn't pull against the cop anymore, and we both fell backward onto the pavement. He dragged me up and threw me into the community garden. I stood up to see both officers assaulting the man while they crammed him into the back of the squad car. The not-Shadow officer turned his head as I was standing, and his eyes flashed a deep red as he grinned slyly. I was still crying. I walked backward into the darkness. At some point, I turned and started to run. It felt like I ran forever, and I don't remember stopping. I woke up the next morning on Grandma Greasy Hinges' floor, caught the bus to the airport, and I haven't been back to L.A. since.

In a lot of ways, I feel like I'm still running. I meet a lot of folks, and I never know how to feel about them. The stares prick me from all angles. I left Alabama a few months ago—headed to Dallas for a new job. I don't really know when I'll go back, but that's okay. I've definitely started over. It's like my eyes are opened to so many things I never thought about before I spent that time in L.A. Still, I never forgave myself for running away from the man when he needed me. I always get the feeling that he would never have run from me. I pray for forgiveness a lot. I just try to do better, and I hope I get it one day. I can see the trees now. They're really quite beautiful if you take a moment to focus on them. Call me crazy. Go ahead, I know you will, but I just want to be a good guy. I want to be somebody's angel.

For The Love of...

"I-I know. I know w-where he is. But I can't take y'all back there, child. If I do, they gon' kill ME, *and* they gon' kill YOU too."

She said this as she fidgeted with her cigarette, nervously. She twirled it between her thumb and forefinger as her eyes darted to the left and right, head drooping, slightly shaking as she mumbled something inaudible. We looked at her for a moment, not quite sure what to say. There was no way we'd find Uncle Sean without her. All of the hope that had welled up in my chest began quickly deflating. I felt my blood pressure dropping, dropping, dropping…

She dropped the cigarette.

It landed in a tiny puddle that was slowly siphoning itself down the sidewalk into a nearby gutter. The ember at the end of the smoke-stick died on impact.

"Shit! That was my last one. Shit. SHIT! Awww, man." Her tremor graduated to an uncontrollable shake. The curses got louder and less comprehensible. Her sudden change in demeanor bewildered those of us in the car. My aunt August revved the engine. I don't think she meant to. Her foot was still on the brake because she knew we had to find Uncle Sean. But her nerves were on that gas pedal, hoping we could get as far away from this crazy lady in this disgusting neighborhood as possible. My mother was the first to speak. Her voice, always mouse-ish, wasn't heard often. Thankfully, it was normally right on time.

"Will you tell us where he is, if we get you more cigarettes?" she squeaked.

The woman looked up, eyes like saucers. A slug's trail of drool slid down her mouth as she approached my car door.

***

"This is as far as I can take you," she said, taking a long drag from her cigarette. She clutched the box of cigarettes in her left hand so hard that it began to bend and crease. Not only had she shown us to Uncle Sean's presumed location, she had given us seemingly every other iota of information she had ever learned. From the story of the first arrest on her record to an overview of care for a marsupial mother's young, a box of cigarettes had granted us an all-access pass into the mind of a crack addict.

"Good luck." she said solemnly. She ran in the opposite direction as fast as she could. I secretly wished I had run away with her.

We stood in the middle of a barren field. Old fast-food bags and cups littered the area, and each patch of grass was opposed by a patch of bare earth of comparable size. The plot was about as big as a soccer field, located deep in the woods behind the housing projects on the back street down which we had initially driven. In the back of the field sat a thirty-foot trailer, a mobile home. Formerly silver, the rust had eaten away at the cheap metal like termites on a log. The brown-orange trailer with a silver top rested in the field: quiet, unbothered, unassuming. A little too unassuming for nothing to be going on inside. We walked right up to the trailer and stood in the path near the doorway. The door creaked open slowly.

My uncle Sean peeked his head out, then scurried down the steps toward my aunt August. He moved furiously, like a mouse in a maze, never quite knowing if forward or left or right was the correct way. His eyes were bloodshot and his pupils dilated. It seemed like he blinked once for every syllable in every word he spoke.

"N-n-n-now A-a-a-ugust, baby..."

I had never seen anything like it in person. She sort of looked like one of the characters, you know, from those fighting games at the arcade. Her hands flew so furiously, I wasn't sure if it was my aunt or a martial artist I was watching. She swung and grunted and grunted and swung, with the occasional whimper. The whimpers were the worst part. She was crying. It hurt her to see my uncle Sean like this. It hurt her to hurt him. Yet she knew that he would never really feel the full extent of the pain she was inflicting on him or the pain she was feeling herself. He was too doped up. My uncle Sean was dying, and my aunt August was trying to beat him back to life. For the love of her husband, she was trying to kill him. She probably figured deep down, it was the best thing for him. And that thought probably made her cry even more.

"Get the hell off me, woman!" my uncle shrieked through the flurry of fists barraging him. "Tonya..." he heaved in-between statements. "Tonya, let's get outta here. C'mon, let's go!"

My mother was Uncle Sean's younger sister and had willingly played the role of his shadow since they were knee high. She was actually the reason we were searching for Uncle Sean. He was supposed to be at her house (because he wasn't allowed at my aunt's house alone), but when she came home, he was gone and so was her car. She checked with Aunt August, and when she realized that Uncle Sean, former military man, was absent without leave, she called me home from school, and my aunt took us straight to the worst part of town. We knew where the drug-laden areas in our city were, even though we had never spent any amount of time there ourselves. An hour and a large box of cigarettes later, and there we were.

"You need help, Sean," my mother murmured. "We can't just leave. We have to take you to get help." Her words were so light— it almost seemed like they got carried off by the South Carolina summer breeze before ever reaching my uncle's ears.

My Uncle Sean wasn't always a crack addict. He had risen through the Army ranks from the time he was a young man into his mid-40s. After finishing a tour in Afghanistan doing intel, he retired from the military. He never liked the politics of the Army. "I don't like having to talk a certain way, or act a certain way just to please somebody else," he used to say. "I just wanna do my job." He had taken a job driving a truck after retiring, moving freight all across the country. The job kept him away from home most of the time and apparently made him the most tired human on Earth. He was liable to fall asleep at any given time, at the drop of a hat. He denied ever having narcolepsy, but his rapid naps were frequent and quick enough that we had thought it necessary to inquire.

We figure he started smoking crack on the road, as dangerous as it sounds. Truck stops host drivers from all over the nation, trading drugs they've picked up in their travels. Somebody probably told him it would help him stay awake long enough to get to the next city. My uncle Sean was simple like that. It wouldn't have taken much more than that to persuade him to try it. Or maybe I just wanted to believe that this whole fiasco was borne out of innocence. Naiveté. Maybe he was always asleep around us because the drugs kept him up all night and beyond when he was on the road. We didn't know. We couldn't know. And that made it even harder for us. Us. Me. My mom. Aunt August. Uncle Sean's three daughters. His four grandkids.

He had been struggling with his addiction behind the veil of a "family secret" for years. He was asked to leave the home he and Aunt August built together. He had started a rehabilitation program but never finished. Everybody kept it quiet, almost like it wasn't happening, all for the love of Aunt August. She was so embarrassed, not only that her husband was addicted to crack cocaine, but that she should be such a good wife to support him through trying to overcome his addiction, when he clearly wasn't trying to overcome his addiction. We pretended to keep her secret because we loved her.

"Don't ever come home," my aunt August said, through teary eyes. "Ever. Don't call me, don't come by, and don't ever try to contact me again." She turned and began walking toward her car. My mom took the car keys from the limp left hand of my uncle Sean. We hustled into the car and sped across the field to catch up with my aunt. When we caught up to her, she wouldn't stop walking. We crept alongside her for maybe fifty yards while she just walked. We could see in the rearview; Uncle Sean stood in the same spot, eyeing us. He grew smaller and smaller in the distance, until we could barely make out his scratching and twitching as he continued to watch us leave. About fifty-five yards out, my aunt dropped to her knees and began sobbing, quietly at first, like a lost child. Then the screams. She screamed and wailed in anguish.

I still get chills down my spine thinking about it, to this day.

We stopped the car and got out. My mother kind of stood over my aunt August while I got down on one knee and rocked her back and forth. Mucus slid out of her nose and her eyes, blood red, continued to pour as she bawled. My aunt cried there on her knees, on a dirt path behind a South Carolina housing project, for what seemed like hours, all for the love of my uncle Sean, the crack addict. It couldn't have been more than twenty minutes, though. Behind us, Uncle Sean had disappeared, probably back into the trailer. We loaded my aunt into the backseat of the car, where she curled up and closed her eyes. The tears squeezed out the corners of her eyes, even with them closed, and slid down her cheeks. She didn't say a word

The Only Sunshine

U *R the only sunshine*

He pressed 'SEND' with his right thumb, his left hand navigating the steering wheel as expertly as an off-hand can. He was long overdue to see Star; it had been weeks since he and his girlfriend were last face to face. Excitement welled in his chest, surged through his core down to his legs. His whole body was so tense, it was too late before he noticed the poorly hidden police vehicle at the intersection ahead. He was in love and living like it. Every thought, every action, every breath—dedicated in some way to the happiness of another. His phone buzzed in his lap. Star responded:

I love you.

***

It started off as a joke, the whole "sunshine" thing. Two years ago, he had been a college basketball player in his last semester, at the end of his career and the edge of the world. He had no clue what to devote his life to after basketball. He honestly wasn't quite sure what else he was good at. Hoops had been putting food on the table and checks in the mail for quite some time. One day, at a volunteer drill camp for kids his team was hosting, he saw her.

Once upon a time, Star Lawson walked down a cloud staircase from Heaven and decided flippantly that she'd make life Hell for men on Earth with her presence alone. She is an angel dipped in beautiful black with the ability to prompt any man who sets sight upon her to ponder his very own existence. *Is there more to life than I once knew? When will I get to experience the finer things? Oh, God! Why hast thou forsaken me?*

Star Lawson is perfect.

He saw her and knew that his key ring of affectionate phrases, sweet nothings, and well-timed touches could unlock everything she had ever hidden away. He knew it would take time. But what is time to a man who holds Heaven in his hands? They exchanged numbers before Star took her nephew home after the camp. He sent her a text.

U were my sunshine today

You see, each day has its own sunshine. Sometimes it's the good news you receive that immediately puts a smile on your face. Other times it's a fond memory of someone or something past. It could even be the summer breeze that, if only for a moment, carries all of your troubles with it to some far-away place. Each day has its own sunshine. Star didn't used to be his sunshine. Not every day. Not in the beginning, when he still had his soul. Other things besides her made him happy. He saw the value in his other relationships and friendships. But after a time, after two years of love and war between him and Star, he was living for her. He rose in the morning and lay to rest at night thinking of her. He made money to take her on romantic outings or maybe surprise her at the office where she worked. The excitement that came with achieving his goals was only exceeded by his excitement at how excited Star would be that achieving his goals put her that much closer to achieving hers.

Pathetic, right? Oh, to be young and in love.

His family felt that his obsession was unhealthy and had removed themselves from the situation. A chorus of Southern niceties, like, "that boy plum crazy over that girl," and "so long as he's happy, I figure he'll be alright," drifted around the room any time the topic was raised. His friends didn't value the struggle of trying to change his mind. He revolved around her like the Earth to the Sun. She was his sunshine. Every day. His only sunshine.

Star greeted him with a soft embrace, a delicate, innocent touch that did little more than excite the mind's eye by alluding to her propensity to touch him in a much, much less innocent way. Her skin felt like satin on his fingertips, and with his head nestled in her freshly washed hair, he noticed she smelled of cherry blossoms, or at least what chemists and cosmetic companies want you to believe cherry blossoms smell like. In her room, they went through a familiar routine, Star disrobing to reveal lace lingerie that was promptly removed by him. She lay back, the hue of her silky, chocolate skin dissolving into her crème colored sheets. He placed the lace panties around his neck, a medal of sorts, before kissing his way from her earlobes to between her thighs. His tongue traversed well-known territory in a different manner each time. He made sure to pleasure her thoroughly before he hoisted himself up, and, meeting her eyes, cleaned his lips with his tongue. She pulled him close and into her, her fingers figure-skating up his back until a deep push by him caused her to dig her nails in. They both moaned softly. Just enough pain to be pleasurable. This was only the beginning. They made love until the sun, too embarrassed to be caught watching outright, crept behind the hills for a more discrete view.

***

He got home, emptied his pockets on the counter (his nightly routine), and headed to his bedroom. The shower he had taken at Star's would ensure he could go straight to sleep, wake up, change, and go to work in the morning. The only light in his bedroom poured through a slim crack in the bathroom door. The shower was running. He undressed and lay down, sleep massaging his eyelids. He had almost faded to the point of no return when he heard, "Who lives on Redland Road?"

His eyes shot open before his body moved. The traffic ticket. The scramble of half-sleep thoughts and potential lies couldn't come together fast enough. He rolled over in the bed and sat up to face her. Her is Tristan. Tristan is his fiancé. Yes, he's engaged.

"She lives over there, doesn't she? You were going to see her."

"There is no her," he said, groggily. "Only you. You are her." His heart beat a thousand times a minute, the standard bpm for compulsive liars.

Tristan got under the covers and turned her back to him. The room was dark and silent. Maybe he was free.

"Who is she?" she said, her words cutting through the silence in the room like an unexpected smoke alarm.

"Tris. There is no she. I was driving around after work, just listening to music. I was going too fast, and I got pulled over. He wrote me a ticket; I stopped at the bar for a second, and then came straight home. Please, babe. I have to work in the morning."

The silence resumed.

Approximately twenty minutes in the house and he was already being interrogated. *Is this what married life is like,* he wondered? The prospect looked grim. The last image he saw was of his alarm clock striking 1:08 a.m. *Great, about five hours to sleep* he thought as he drifted away once more. On the other side of the bed, Tristan let the crumpled traffic ticket fall from her left hand onto the floor. In the space where the officer had filled out the details of the infraction, the "Time of Offense" read 7:38 p.m.

***

His head was pounding. His thoughts, a tornado in a tin can. His trembling hands shuddered involuntarily; the rest of him was paralyzed. His mouth dry, his palms sweaty, he read the text again.

I think I might be pregnant

He had no clue what to say. He hadn't spoken to his fiancé in three or four days when the text message came through. There was no context, no further investigation, just speculation. He sent a text message to Star.

Sunshine, I need U

He got his things together and went straight to her house without waiting for her response.

He always talked to Star about his relationship issues. When they had first started fooling around, she had a boyfriend, and he, of course, had Tristan. They both agreed that they would keep things light, take the pressure off each other. And then they fell in love. Star's boyfriend had fallen by the wayside some time ago. They lasted a standard duration for early twenties relationships in this day and age. But he and Tristan had known each other since high school. She had been with him through the ups and downs of his sports injuries, consistent flings with campus groupies, threats to revoke his scholarship, his mother's health problems—everything. He felt obligated to repay her for her dedication by promising her better years than those behind them. But he wasn't ready. They both knew it but couldn't bring themselves to accept it.

Tristan was the usual suspect for a woman who sticks around long after she should have gone. Her father, a philanderer much like her fiancé, had mistreated her mother for years and years until one day everything stopped. Everything literally stopped.

He went to prison.

Nothing related to the mother though, something about a corporate embezzlement scandal. Tristan couldn't remember, she was too young at the time, and her mother never spoke about it. Tristan's mother raised three children for ten years all alone and never so much as batted an eyelash at another man. When Tristan's father was released, he found himself in the loving care of his fast-forwarded family. Her mother would steal a glance across the dinner table at him while he scarfed down his food like he missed the message that the prospect of a "last-meal" was null and void. She would smirk, mostly behind her lips, and be happy. Happy because she got the man she wanted. But even happier that nobody else got to have him.

He and Star talked for hours once he got there. Really, he talked for hours. All the stress, uncertainty, worry, upset (typical things that come with getting your fiancé pregnant, right?) flowed out of him, into the room, and out of the open window by the standing lamp in the corner. When he had expended all of his negative energy, he sat on the bed next to Star and looked out the window. He pulled her close to him and ran his fingers through her hair.

"You know I love you. Things have never really been ideal, but...I'm just trying to make sure this doesn't come between us. I always want to be with you. No matter what. You know that? You know that."

Star gazed out of the window. The sky was dark. No stars.

"Babe..."

"I'm pregnant."

She was even farther along than Tristan was.

Star put her face in her hands, and with his arms around her body, he could feel the tension deflate from her in its entirety. He lay back and pulled her into his chest. She curled up close to him. The house was silent for the next hour, excluding the periodic deliveries of the icemaker in the freezer in the kitchen. He heard her crying softly into his T-shirt and felt her rubbing her face against his chest to wipe the tears. He couldn't bring himself to look down at her. He wished the ice-maker would be a little louder.

"I...I promise you...I promise you that I'm going to be here for whatever you need. And there's no way I would ever abandon my ch—,"

"It might not be yours," Star said, tensing up once again.

The room went hazy. The ice-maker rumbled again.

***

He had never imaged Star could be unfaithful. What irony, right? Eventually, she got tired of being the getaway. It's like being trapped on an island. At first, it's beautiful. Who cares that you can't get home? You've got the sun and the water, and you're miles away from all your worries. Unfortunately, you're also miles away from all the things you've ever loved, potentially with no way to return. Star grew tired of being the safe-haven after he argued with Tristan. She hated never expressing emotions because "side-chicks" weren't supposed to cause problems. He had asked her never to feel, without so many words. She had relinquished her right to all the parts of a relationship that made people fight to keep them alive, for better or for worse. She had taken the easiest thing in the world and made it difficult. And she didn't care because she deserved to be happy.

He was laying on his back shooting his basketball up close to the ceiling and then catching it as it came down. His mind was always clear on the court. Basketball was so woven into his DNA that it required very little mental effort. A visceral experience. He missed the days when how to defeat the crosstown rival was amongst the largest of problems he had. *What would a good man do?* He wondered as he continued to "shoot" the ball, on autopilot. He had never considered himself a good man. He had good qualities, but he was selfish. People always said real men put their families first and could bear any burden with the utmost strength, no matter how heavy. He remembered having stood at the door behind his mother's leg after she backed his father out of the house, nose bloody, shakily gripping the pistol she kept beneath the spare sheets in the closet. There hadn't been much opportunity to learn about manhood from his father-figure after that, assuming he had any lessons to offer that didn't pertain to domestic abuse. His conception of manhood came from his friends, his boys, who were no older than he was. The lives they dreamed of and eventually built, fueled by hip-hop culture and illusions of grandeur, low community expectations and misplaced praise, were coming to an early end. Townsmen of a stiller town, they had never thought to plan past twenty-five.

He was scared. Of everything, but mainly of losing Tristan. He knew he had made a grave mistake. Thoughts of Star brought on bouts of anger and embarrassment. Thoughts of Tristan, guilt. He knew what he had to do. He wasn't just sure. He was positive.

***

"I'm not pregnant."

She cried. He cried too, but he wasn't sure why. He had showed up at Tristan's apartment around 9:30 p.m., slightly tipsy and emotionally vulnerable. He told her everything. He told her about Star, and the baby, and the "other guy," and how he had never wanted anything more in life than he wanted a second chance with her, Tristan. He cried and paced and talked until he hardly made sense. It was really an Oscar-worthy performance, the kind of thing you see at the end of a film that makes you think, "Yeah, they're going to win something for this." He didn't so much run out of words to say as he did breath to say them with. While he was rubbing his eyes during intermission, Tristan broke the news.

"I'm not pregnant."

Thank the Lord for false positives.

When the doctor had disconfirmed Tristan's greatest joy and worst fear, she had been inconsolable. The doctor had awkwardly patted her on the back, blind to the exact source of her anguish.

Of course, through teary eyes and salt-trailed cheeks, Tristan had promised herself she would "hold him down no matter what." At the time, she had no idea that the possibilities of "no matter what" entailed an illegitimate child from an illicit relationship. But hey, a promise is a promise.

"You're the only sunshine I've got," he said, his face muffled in Tristan's neck.

They cried and cuddled and cried until they fell asleep like two babies, each the other's primary caregiver.

***

"I think she's gonna keep it, man...fuck...she's gonna keep it."

"That bitch is crazy," Alisha said through the phone.

He had to chuckle. Her Texas twang made offhand comments like that so much funnier. He had always loved how much of a straight-shooter Alisha was. She was all about getting down to the root of the problem and moving on with her life. *So, what are we doing? 'Cause I don't really have time to play around.* He had told her numerous times that she should make shirts with the question on the front, the following phrase on the back. She'd make a killing solely off peers wanting to buy them in friendly spite of her.

Alisha was the Star before Star, back when he was being recruited. The sex was like fireworks. They were young and inexperienced, lacking in many ways, but passion wasn't one. They had always kept their relationship casual (sexual). They had both been in relationships as long as they had known each other and had agreed that there was no reason to disturb each other's lives in that way. In fact, when he had dumped his old girlfriend and started dating Tristan, Alisha would still ask questions about his "girlfriend." She had no idea she wasn't asking about the same person until he told her about their engagement. They laughed about it in her downtown Dallas condo as she straddled him and ran her nails down his chest and abs. They were great friends.

He had enlisted the help of Alisha a couple of weeks after his fresh start with Tristan. Star had called and told him she wanted to schedule an abortion but that she was scared and didn't know how. Of course, now that he was a good man, he agreed not only to set it up for her, but to accompany her to the clinic on the day of the procedure. Of course, he knew nothing about clinics or abortions, so he asked Alisha for help doing all the things he had agreed to do. He had to lean on Alisha quite a bit throughout this entire affair. Star would hardly talk to him, and every time he tried to vent about the situation to Tristan, she would cry and get angry. Alisha had really saved him emotionally and logistically, and for that, he would forever be thankful.

He sat in the dark lobby of the cold clinic, waiting for Star. She was a little late, but that was normal. He put his face in his hands and remembered the night it all happened. The sloppy, drunk kisses, fumbling to get each other's clothes off, and the 90s R&B playing through the walls in the living room as they felt the electricity pass between each other's bodies. He pleased her with his tongue for what felt like forever. When she couldn't take it anymore, she clawed at his back and softly moaned, "I want it." He brought his face up and smirked. He raised himself off the bed and went to retrieve his only condom from his pants pocket.

"What are you doing?"

This was a fair question. They hadn't used condoms since their third or fourth time being together. But something had moved him to grab protection before they started this time. What exactly? He didn't know.

"Are we good?"

"Yeah," he responded. "I mean, I'm good. Are you good?"

"Of course I'm good," she snapped.

"Nah, I mean like, with the birth control and everything."

"Whyyyy, are you asking this nowwwww?" Star said exasperated. "I actually just stopped taking my bc, because I'm switching to a new kind next week. But I can't get pregnant. I literally just stopped taking it yesterday."

"So what if you get pregnant?"

"I won't. You're really killing my whole vibe right now, for your information."

"But what if you do?"

"I won't! Shit, if I do, I'll take care of it, okay? Come here..."

She pulled him close, tightening her grip and gasping as he entered her. Ecstasy. Pleasure.

"Excuse me, sir?"

He took his face out of his hands and looked up. The desk assistant at the clinic was beckoning him over.

"So the woman you're waiting on is an hour late, and we're closing soon. If she doesn't get here in the next five minutes or so, we won't be able to see her."

"I'll try to get a hold of her," he said, cotton-mouthed.

He had called Star eleven times before he realized she wasn't coming.

Fuck.

Star pulled a no-show at one other abortion appointment. She had resurfaced a week or so after the first missed appointment, apologizing and explaining how she was sick and scared and and and and and. She said she had heard of a really good clinic in Southern California from her cousin and that she would feel most comfortable doing it there. She hadn't been feeling well, though, and would need to fly as opposed to driving all that way. He had scraped up money to fly her there, and he would drive. He had tossed two chairs in the waiting room and was working on a third before security had to detain him. Her excuse after that one was that she had never flown and got cold feet about the plane at the last minute. Then she disappeared again.

"That bitch is really crazy," Alisha said. "Call me when you hear from her, though; you know I'll do what I can. If she wasn't so far along, I'd have my little cousins rough her ass up."

He had to chuckle. He hung up the phone, head pounding. Back to real life. The rain came down hard outside. He lay down and let the pane percussion play him to sleep.

***

He was watching reality TV when he got the call. Tristan lay curled up in his lap, her fuzzy, pink socks a pop of color against the navy couch. He had spoken to Alisha that morning for about an hour and cleared his mind, so he and Tristan were having a good day. It had been raining every day for almost a month, so an intimate day in was really the best option. No fights, no drama. Just serenity and bad TV. He didn't even mind too much about the TV, as long as Tristan was happy. The two of them were supposed to go to her parents' house later. It would be like in the beginning where he was still "the boyfriend." They would have him over for dinner, Tristan's mother happy to dote and wait on someone as an example of the dedication needed to catch and keep a man, her father completely ensnared in the nostalgia of basketball stories, reliving his glory days against the end-table defenders and droves of adoring, throw-pillow fans. His phone vibrated on the ottoman.

The contact name read "My Shining Star." He still hadn't changed her name in his phone.

"Are you going to answer it?" Tristan asked.

"...I guess I should."

He dislodged himself from Tristan's grip, scooped up his phone, and went into the bedroom. He stared out the window at the steady downpour.

"Hello?"

"Hey. Um...I just wanted to tell you that we're keeping it."

"Huh? What? We? Who is we?"

"I don't really want to talk long. I'm just trying to move on with my life. We is me and my boyfriend. The father of my child."

"Star, you told me that it was just as possible for him to b-"

"I know, but my point is...no matter who the biological father is, I want to be with my boyfriend. We're going to get married. He will accept and raise this child as his own no matter what."

"So that's it? You just never talk to me again? That's not right, Star. I don't care that you don't care; if that's my child, I need to know. I'm going to do right by it. By her."

"It's going to be a boy. You're making this difficult. We're happy. Why can't you just leave us alone?"

"It's not right to leave my child to be taken care of by another man. I have to know."

"It's not your child."

"Fuck, Star. Come on!" His palm left a condensation fossil on the cold, glass pane. "We're about five months out. You don't have to talk to me at all until then. But I need to know when the baby is born, and I need to know if it's mine. Don't disappear on me."

"I don't know. Look, I'll be around okay? I have to go."

"Star. Star!"

He glanced at his phone screen only to see his home screen. The call had ended. "Everything okay, babe?" echoed through the hallway into his bedroom from the living room. He looked out the window again. The rain had stopped, and the clouds had broken. Rays of light shined through some of them, the way Heaven looks whenever it's printed or drawn or something. The clouds drifted slowly in different directions, each headed to rest after a depletive outpouring, like when the funeral is over, but the true mourning has yet to begin. The sun shined, for the first time in a while

A nd now, what you've all been waiting for—the man behind the success of the Academy Award-nominated film, *Distinction*, Dr. Elan Zola!"

Mack Morristerr's voice drowned in a sea of applause. The applause was so loud it felt muffled inside Dr. Zola's ears. He knew the cheering was louder than it sounded to him, so he rubbed his ears fiercely before he took his first steps out on to the stage. The sweat from his palms made his ears moist, but still the clapping sounded like rain on a rooftop. His eyes adjusted painfully as the fulgent stage beams enveloped him. As he reached to shake Mack Morristerr's hand, the silence rushed out of the massive auditorium like an untied balloon. It hadn't looked like 2,000 people. But it definitely sounded like 2,000 people.

"Dr. Zola! So happy to have you," Mack Morristerr grinned. "I think you're the first doctor I've ever had on my show. Probably because I was nervous I'd finally be confirmed to be looney."

The drummer played a sting, and the crowd laughed politely.

"What kind of doctor are you exactly?"

"I am a doctor of psychology."

"Interesting. It took you years to get to that level of education I presume?"

"Yes, it was quite the journey."

"But it has all paid off, as we can tell by your success not only in your field, but by your contributions to the arts. You were a creative consultant for the movie *Distinction*, out on DVD and

Blu-Ray right now folks, that did record numbers at the box office. Some are calling it the best movie of our generation, and word among the cast is that you're the man whose insights really brought the story to life. We'll talk more about that in a second, but first let's take a look at this clip from the film."

The lights dimmed, and Dr. Zola looked down at his shoes. He heard the clip start, the main character's raspy voice solidly delivering a line that Dr. Zola remembered him choking over two hundred times before nailing. *Distinction* was a movie about a world in which people with pronounced psychological disorders—delirium, schizophrenia, OCD, various phobias—have to collaborate in a not-quite-post-apocalyptic world to rebuild society and humanity while fending off the last wave of dangerous threats to the remaining humans.

The catch is that the people trying to save the world in the movie, people who most consider unable to live normal, safe lives in today's world, are actually only a projection of what human life will become. The rationale is that the same destructive human behavior that brought about the beginning of the apocalypse actually created the stress and environmental factors that evolved (or devolved) the human race to the point where most people developed some sort of advanced psychological disorder. So, while it's very much a film about togetherness, perseverance, and sensitivity to the human condition, it's also a cautionary tale and a reminder that as humans continue to make what they call advancements, they are also destroying and erasing much of what they need to preserve stable life on Earth. The director is quoted as saying the movie is meant to get the point across that "...we're not as smart as we think we are. We're not as in control as we think we are. We're not as distinct as we think we are."

But as Dr. Zola looked at his shoes, and the lights began to awaken, he did not care about any of that. He did not fancy social theory. He wasn't very fond of *Distinction*. He didn't care about Mack Morristerr. He cared about his son. He missed his son.

"Very thought-provoking stuff. I haven't seen the movie yet, but I simply *must* make time this weekend; it looks amazing, wouldn't you all say so?" Mack Morristerr encouraged.

The crowd roared.

"So, Dr. Zola. How do you, as a doctor of psychology, get involved with helping to essentially co-direct a film?"

This wasn't the part of the story Dr. Zola wanted to tell. He had never done an interview before. He didn't have a publicist. Nobody had advised him to screen Mack Morristerr's questions.

"Um...I...so..."

Dr. Zola rubbed his chin. Mack cocked his head in confusion.

"Feels weird to be on the couch and have me asking you questions, huh Dr. Zola?" he chuckled. The crowd laughed heartily. "But seriously, did they source from various psychologists in the area, did you apply, what happened that made this possible?"

"I'm not a psychiatrist."

Mack's eyes darted nervously. "Huh?"

"You said it feels weird for me to be on the couch answering questions—like a role reversal. But I'm not a psychiatrist. I don't do that."

Mack's eyes flashed angrily for half a second before his on-screen etiquette reactivated.

"Oh! My apologies, so—"

"Dakota and I—" Dr. Zola started.

"Dakota? You mean the late Dakota Abrams, the original director of *Distinction* whose untimely death before filming started shocked and saddened Hollywood? A real pioneer."

"Yes. Dakota. Um…Dakota and I were old friends. Good friends."

Dr. Zola paused for a second. He wasn't sure why.

"Well, um. Dakota had asked me to help with the film. We hadn't talked in years. A decade really. But he called one day and asked me to help him on set. He was a brilliant man, truly. But he, uh…never had much of a memory," Dr. Zola chuckled. "Well, I declined politely. I told him that Hollywood was no place for me. I've got a young son, Elijah. Besides, I hardly know anything about movies. He seemed pretty sad about it, but I think he understood….when he passed though, everyone was devastated. I went to the funeral, and his family told me about how he always talked about me. I mean, sheesh, I hadn't talked to Dakota for ten years, but you'd think we were still in college the way his folks acted. It was nice. They're nice people. Hello to you all, if you're watching. Well, they said he had told them about how disappointed he was that I couldn't help with the movie. And I figured, you know, he had been such a great friend to me you know? And he had so much faith in this project. I knew I couldn't do it justice, but I just...I don't know...I figured a shot at it was the least I could do, to pay my respects...and to honor a good friend."

"Wow. That is *truly* amazing. I'm sure his family appreciates such a kind gesture, and I know he's looking down smiling at how great the film turned out."

Dr. Zola felt bashful.

"...and probably at all that money it made too!"

Another sting, more laughs.

"But I have to ask. You said Mr. Abrams had a bad memory. So, he wanted you on set to help remind him of his ideas for the movies? Had he told you these ideas previously? You two hadn't spoken in years...what were you reminding him of?"

Dr. Zola was quiet for a moment. He tried to think of a way to answer the question that wouldn't create any new questions.

"Um. He didn't so much want me to remind him of ideas or an event, but feelings. I guess it all stretches back to our last spring break in college?"

"Spring break?!?" Mack squealed.

The crowd laughed hysterically.

"The doctor had a wild side, uh-oh, look out! Okay, we'll follow up with that after a word from our sponsors. Check out *Distinction*, out now on DVD and Blu-Ray."

Dr. Zola exhaled heavily. He hadn't even realized that he had been holding his breath. He knew the time would come eventually when he would have to tell this story, and although he hadn't foreseen it happening that night, he figured it was just as good a time as any. He thought of Elijah. Yes, just as good a time as any. And it would be recorded. Broadcast nationally and recorded. Maybe, hopefully...he'd never have to tell it again.

***

We rode down to the beach. There were eight of us in total. Dakota, myself, a couple of our other buddies, and four girls. Oddly enough, we didn't know the girls. The morning we left—it was a Monday—they saw us packing the van outside our dorm. I think they stayed in the next dorm over. They seemed nice enough, and they had gas money—one thing we didn't have enough of. Dakota and I were so confused about why four white girls would feel comfortable crossing state lines to vacation with us. They didn't even know us. But, like I said, they seemed nice enough. We didn't mind. It was college. It was spring break.

The ride down and the first day went off without a hitch. We had drinks by the beach; we even swam a little. I knew my girlfriend, Elijah's mother now, was there, but I hadn't seen her. We weren't on the best terms. She had come down separately with her friends. Still, we had a great time enjoying the sun, talking, and laughing with our crew.

At some point Dakota and I broke off from the group—I don't remember why. But while we were away, we met these two girls. And, man...who knows what they really looked like, but in that moment...they were the most beautiful girls we had ever seen. And boy, were they into us. I mean laying it on thick. They invited us to a club on the strip that night and told us after the club we could hang out at their place. We could hardly wait.

The club was a sweaty place. The air tasted like salt, and I couldn't tell if it was from the ocean breeze blowing through the rickety building or the mass of bodies vibrating all throughout it. Dakota was by the bar most of the night talking to a blonde. I couldn't bring myself to flirt with another woman in public, knowing my girlfriend could be around any corner at any moment. I am somewhat ashamed to admit, though, that all my thoughts were focused on the girl I had met on the beach earlier. I couldn't wait to leave the club to see her again...to touch her...to feel the heat flow between our bodies as we anticipated each other's next move. I was completely trapped in my mind.

Dakota got a call from his beach girl around three a.m. Excitement welled up inside me as he ended the call, telling her that we'd be at their hotel in fifteen minutes. We pushed through the crowd of sweaty people to the door. Once outside, Dakota started to pull up a GPS app on his phone—we weren't quite sure what direction the beach girls' hotel was in. I closed my eyes and let the beach breeze wash over me. The cool night air was a nice contrast to the hot, sticky feeling the anticipation of our rendezvous had given me. I opened my eyes and used the bottom of my shirt to wipe my face. As I angled my head downward I noticed something glimmering against the dark pavement.

I bent down and picked up a phone. It was a Saturn 5. I recognized it because I used to have one; I had switched to the Saturn 6 months earlier. I noticed that the phone still had battery life, and as Dakota began nudging me to walk east, I decided to be a Good Samaritan. I was in such a good mood; we'd be laying with beautiful women in a matter of minutes, and I figured why not go for some good karma. I told Dakota to wait. I had decided that before we visited our beach girls, I would return this phone to its rightful owner. It was what I would want someone to do for me.

That was my first mistake.

"You ready? Their hotel is like, five minutes that way," Dakota pointed toward the pier.

"Hold on, I found this phone. I want to try to give it back to the owner."

"What? Who's the owner?"

"Well, I don't know…"

"Okay…so how—never mind. Look, we should just go to the hotel!"

As I started to respond, I felt the phone vibrate in my hand. I looked down and saw an incoming call from "Emily" onscreen.

"Haha, check it out," I said, showing Dakota the phone. "Maybe it's the owner."

"Or maybe it's just Emily."

I answered the phone. The voice on the other end sounded incredibly relieved. I explained that I had found the phone on the ground outside of the club and that we were hoping to return it back to its owner. Emily asked where we were and said they'd be right there. Ten minutes later, she called again.

"Hi, where are you again?"

"We're still right outside the club, waiting for you guys. Are you close?"

"Yes, we'll be there soon."

Dakota was unhappy at this point. He figured we were missing our chance with the beach babes, but I tried to reassure him that not much time had actually passed. We waited another twenty minutes or so, and Dakota decided he was through with me. I had annoyed him to the point of silence. When he stopped talking to me, I decided to scroll through the recovered phone. I went into the text messages, and the first one was from Emily, about an hour prior.

To whoever finds this phone and returns to the owner, there will be a $500 reward. Please call Emily at...

I didn't read the rest. I tugged at Dakota until he had no choice but to read the screen I was thrusting into his face. He looked at the phone, then at me, then the phone, then at me. He smiled. We had probably mentally spent about half of the reward money when the phone rang again.

"Hi, are you still outside the club?"

The question was puzzling this time.

"Yes, but we actually have to go soon. We've been waiting for a while an—,"

"What do you have on?"

"Um...a white shirt. Black jeans and sneakers. Oh, and a blue cap. Are you here? Can you see me?"

I got no response.

"Hello? Hello?"

I looked at the phone and saw that the call had ended. I wasn't sure if it dropped or if Emily had ended the call.

We waited for about five more minutes. I felt a bit nauseated. A strong, salty breeze stung my eyes, and when I finished rubbing them, I noticed a parade of blue and red lights through my bleary vision. All of a sudden, two policemen rushed Dakota and me. Their guns were drawn, and I remember stumbling backward with my hands in front of my face as they charged us. The white policeman holstered his gun and grabbed me by the wrist with his left hand and the front of my shirt with the other hand. He leaned his weight against me and drove me to the ground. The phone flew out of my hand and bounced on the pavement. My back hit the pavement too, hard. The cop turned me over and began to handcuff me. I screamed a bunch of things I probably would be embarrassed to repeat.

Out of the corner of my eye, I saw Dakota on the ground too. We were both face down. The Hispanic policeman was pushing the side of Dakota's face into the pavement while he blabbered some gibberish into his walkie-talkie. I could tell Dakota wanted to cry, but he wouldn't. His eyes were pink and watery, his breaths short and forced.

"Get off his head!" I screamed at the Hispanic officer.

"Shut up!" the white officer screamed back at me.

Still, I saw Dakota's officer ease some of the tension off of his head and neck. After about five minutes, they pulled us up onto our feet. We were surrounded by a crowd of people who had watched the entire thing. Some were filming it with their phones. I started yelling obscenities at my officer again, demanding to know what we did and why they were treating us like this. Neither officer answered but instead continued to walk us across the road to where they had parked the cop cars. We passed a street vendor who was selling hot dogs. He started playing the "Bad Boys" TV show theme on a portable radio as the cops walked us past his grill. I thrashed and screamed, "Fuck you!" as we passed the grill and tried my hardest to kick it over. My policeman tightened the cuffs and wrestled me back down to my knees. Eventually, we began walking again. As we approached, three white girls—spring breakers—leaned up against the cop car.

Dakota's officer handed one of the girls the phone I had dropped. The three of them huddled around it, examining it.

"What the hell is wrong with you!?" I yelled.

My officer told me to shut-up for the thousandth time.

"Officer, they stole our phone. Completely stole it. Thank you. Thank you for giving it back. We just didn't know what to do without it, and...and I'm so so glad we have it now."

The girl speaking, I assumed it was Emily, was slurring her words terribly. She and both of her friends had glassy eyes and swayed a little too hard in the light ocean breeze.

"They're drunk! We didn't steal anything!"

"You had the phone when we found you, Son." my officer said.

"We found it outside the club! It was on the ground. I was trying to return it to its owner. We waited. We waited almost an hour for Emily to come and get it! Let us go! Why would I steal that phone? It's a Saturn 5. Check my pockets; I *own* a Saturn 6!"

"It's not my job to know why criminals commit crimes, Son. Just to catch 'em."

My ears got hot, and my heart pounded in my chest. I started screaming again and could feel myself going hoarse from overexertion. The girls thanked the officers and walked away. The farther they got, the more my anger was replaced by fear. We were really being arrested. My throat got dry, and my stomach felt light. I looked at Dakota, and by the way he looked back at me, I could tell he felt the same. He had scratches all over the right side of his face from the pavement. They sat us in the back of the Hispanic officer's car. I was happy that they put us together and happy that they didn't put us with the white cop. We sat cuffed in the backseat while he typed up the report.

My head was pounding. I didn't know whether it was fear or bodily injury that was making it hard for me to breathe, but I measured my breaths out—short and calculated. Dakota was crying, silently. His head tilted back and rested on the seat as the tears slid down his cheeks. At the time, I was scared, but I kept waiting to wake up. I believed in the good of the world. I truly thought that as long as I didn't do anything bad, nothing bad would happen to me. It was the reason I tried to return the phone in the first place. As I sat in the backseat of the squad car, I just kept thinking it would all end any second, that the officer would say, "my mistake, this isn't right," and we would be free to go. I kept waiting, but it never happened. I leaned to the right and peered over the officer's shoulder as he typed.

"Hey...Hey!! What are you writing? That isn't the truth! That doesn't even make any sense!!"

The report was a lie. It stated that Dakota and I had met these girls in the club around 11:30. After approaching them to dance and being turned down, Dakota and I had (indescribably) stolen the phone and exited the club. The girls had searched for the phone for the next three hours apparently, until calling it and catching us "red handed" with the phone; at which point, we attempted to extort them for five hundred dollars in exchange for the phone. The girls contacted the authorities after agreeing to our proposed deal, and they lulled us to sleep outside the club until the officers could move in and apprehend us.

Bull. Shit.

Nothing was true. Dakota and I hadn't even got to the club until one a.m. None of these blondes was the one Dakota had spent time talking to, and frankly none of them was cute. Honestly, they were all unattractive, homely even. I wouldn't have danced with any of them. How dare they think we'd be so mad at getting turned down by them that we'd steal their stuff in some pathetic ploy for revenge? The thought infuriated me. The police took a story from three drunk, lonely girls and arrested us based on its perceived validity. Because black boys lust for white women. Black boys steal things. We may not know much, but this we know.

"None of that is true!"

"Oh yeah?" the officer asked.

My breath stopped short at the sight of hope.

"Sir. I'm as serious as I've ever been. That story is a lie, and I can tell you what really happened."

"You will. As soon as we get to the station."

My heart dropped. The officer pulled out of the club parking lot area, which had since become empty with the dispersal of patrons. We said good-bye to the spring break metropolis as we drove through miles and miles of marsh and wood, headed toward the county jail. I started crying quietly, and I wondered if Dakota was still crying. I couldn't see him in the dark of night. All of this was my fault. I had wanted to return the phone, and now he and I were going to jail hundreds of miles away from home. Neither of us had ever been in any trouble.

We got locked up on a Wednesday. I'll never forget. My inmate number was 1357008. We were booked on grand theft and extortion. They put us in Cell 38 of the Atlantis 4 building, Block D.

At least they let us stay together.

Before that though, we checked in and swapped our street clothes for prison uniforms. The correctional officers lead us to a bathroom where we could wash and change, but I didn't want to shower in jail. I ran the water and changed clothes without ever getting wet. They stuck us in a holding cell with about fifteen other inmates. Neither one of us was offered the chance to make a phone call. We tried to stay together in a corner of the holding cell, but the inmates surrounded us. It was protocol to scope out the new guy. Knowing your environment was essential behind bars. There was no hiding.

"What are you in for?" one lanky inmate asked. He had open sores on his neck and chest. Some of them obscured parts of tattoos that comprised his body mural. His hair was long and smelled like wet dirt right after rain, like he had climbed out of the ground.

"They arrested us for stealing a phone. But we didn't steal anything."

Now, you'd think jail is like the movies where after one person says they're innocent, every inmate in the entire building starts a cacophony of innocence pleas. But that wasn't the case. The inmates were all extremely intrigued by our story. Most of them were admittedly guilty, and although they noted that this particular jail was where most of the mischievous spring-breakers ended up, none of them could recall a time where someone in there was arrested in the manner that we were. Even the correctional officers who overheard our story could be heard whispering "sheesh" and "that doesn't sound right" across the room at the intake desk. But, for as much sympathy as they may have had for us, none of them offered us any help.

In the holding cell with us there was OJ, a twenty-year-old troublemaker who had walked into an assisted living home and discharged a fire extinguisher. He claimed he thought it would be funny to watch the "old frosties slip and slide." Darren had assaulted his wife during an argument about dinner. Avery was in for battery—he wouldn't describe the charge, but he was a first-time inmate. The jagged, fresh gash that climbed from his left eyebrow past his hairline made Dakota and me think that the other person in that fight probably didn't fare too well if Avery was the one in jail with an injury like that. There was also Dog. Nobody knew his real name yet—he had just come to the jail. The urban legend that followed Dog was that he had committed a string of violent crimes up and down the coast. He had already served time at two prisons, and he was just stopping over here. He would soon be transported to another prison in another state to serve a ten-year sentence. Nobody doubted that Dog was the type of man who could kill a person. He was massive, maybe six feet four inches or six feet five inches, and even though he had terrible posture, he cut an imposing figure. His face remained in a rigid scowl the entire time the other inmates relayed his story to us. He never interjected, so we assumed it was all true.

Lastly, there was Mikey. Sometimes truth can be stranger than fiction. Our first interaction went something like this.

"What'd they book ya on?"

"Grand theft, extortion...you?"

"Grand theft. Haha...right on, man. What'd ya take?"

"Well...I didn't take anything. I'm innocent."

"Shit, man. That sucks. I'm not!" he said, letting out a hearty laugh.

"Ha. Well, yeah. We're going to get out of here. We just need one of these correctional officers to hear us out."

"Us?"

"Yeah," I pointed to Dakota in the corner talking to the lanky worm inmate.

"Oh, okay. Thought maybe ya had one a those multiple personality things happenin'. But shit, man. The C.O.s can't do shit for ya. The judge don't work again 'til Friday. You'll be here until at least then. And hell, if he don't make it down the list to you on Friday, you'll be here over the weekend too."

My mouth got dry again. "So you mean, like...you mean we'll just be here? With no way to even talk to somebody about leaving?"

"Dude, that's what jail is!" He laughed again. "But ya can talk all you want. Can't nobody set ya free 'cept the judge."

"And he won't be here until Friday...?"

"Mhm."

My heart was heavy in my chest. The situation seemed to get worse and worse. In that moment, I felt mostly for Dakota. He wouldn't even be here if it wasn't for me. I had gotten us stuck here for days. I wasn't sure how we'd make it.

"Hell ya, Man. I hope I can get out Friday too. The li'l phone I stole wasn't even worth much. Didn't get to keep the piece of shit long either. Couldn't even make my getaway before I got caught." He let out another laugh.

I almost didn't catch it.

"I'm sorry. You said...you stole a phone? That's why you're in here?"

"Yep, sure did."

"When did this happen?

"Aw, hell. Not long ago. Little while, maybe four p.m. or five p.m. I was high, man, I really didn't check the clock."

"You robbed someone? Or did you find the phone?"

"Ehhh, somewhere in between, I guess. It was kinda just sittin' there, ya know? Maybe it was lost, and I found it, haha. Or maybe it wasn't!"

My mind started swirling with a thousand possibilities. I tried to piece together what it all meant.

"What kind of phone did you steal?"

"Man. It was a Bluebird. Sweet little phone. The older version though, which is why I figured it wasn't worth much. Probably could have wiped it and pawned it down on LeSalle though."

It all meant nothing.

As my spirit was broken for the third time that day, one of the C.O.s stepped into the holding cell.

"Salvador, you're up. It's time to go. The rest of you get ready for bed. Salvador, come to the front. You're outta here."

The man called Salvador walked to the front of the cell and stopped right in front of Dakota and me. He was a small, hairy man with shifty eyes. He turned and exited the cell. As he passed by, the smell of sweat hung in the air. He and the C.O. were gone for about fifteen minutes. They were leading Salvador out of the jail when he stopped in front of the holding cell again.

"Cell phone boys. Yoo-hoo! Cell phone boys."

Dakota and I looked at each other.

"Yes, yes, you, you. Come."

I was hesitant at first, but I watched as Dakota walked up to him and peered through the bars. I followed closely behind.

"Heard your story. Bad, bad s-story. I-I'm leaving, but I-I can...I can call w-whoever you need me to, and let them know you're here. You are here. I can let them know."

It seemed like an empty promise. Everything I had put faith in that day had betrayed me. I wasn't interested in this stuttering, sweaty man and his offer. He could barely speak. I almost felt like he was mocking us.

"Just g-give me number. I'll tell 'em your story. Bad, bad story. I will. I'll tell 'em."

"We would really appreciate that."

They were the first words I had actually heard Dakota say since we had been arrested. He sounded so calm and resilient. A wave of guilt rushed over me. Here I was, a mess, especially so because I had put my friend in such a terrible situation. And he was handling it better than me.

Salvador got a pen and a scrap of paper from the intake desk and scribbled down both my father's and Dakota's father's numbers.

He turned one last time before he left the jail and said, "I'll tell 'em."

They filed us out of the holding cell and down the hall. I saw *Atlantis 4* carved into a large, stone wall on the way to our cells. I wasn't sure if the jail was Atlantis or if we were in the fourth Atlantis building. I didn't even know what county I was in. But I never forgot that wall.

They put Dakota and me in the same cell, like I mentioned before. The cots were thin, and the blankets felt like they were made from lint. It was so cold that first night. I shivered for a while before I could fall asleep. Just as I was dozing off, I heard a sound. It seemed like it was coming from a couple cells down. I craned my neck in the dark to try to hear more clearly what was happening.

It was a whimper.

Somebody was crying, softly at first, barely sniffling. But for the next hour, the entire block remained silent as the crying became louder and louder, eventually graduating to screams. It was really a harrowing sound. There, in the dark, someone was losing it. The realization that the very fibers of his existence were coming undone had taken control of his emotions. It was starting to sink in that he might not ever be free again.

But I didn't care. How dare he sit yards away from me, crying, when he was probably guilty for whatever he was in here for? Meanwhile, Dakota and I were trapped in this place where we didn't belong. I had no remorse for him. I thought about calling out to quiet him down several times. But I didn't. The longer he cried, the angrier I got. My nerves were on end. I did push-ups until I couldn't feel my arms, trying to make myself more tired than anxious about being in jail so that I could sleep. I fell asleep but woke up every two hours with a start and resumed my push-up routine until I passed out again. Morning came in what seemed like minutes.

After the morning shower (which I skipped, covering myself with my towel in the corner the entire time), they herded us aggressively toward the cafeteria. They were loud and physical with us, making sure we walked quietly and in line. They hadn't been this harsh the night before. One inmate had tried to be rebellious, refusing to walk single file on his path to the caf and pushing his way out of line. An officer jacked the inmate up against the wall and jammed his forearm into his neck. He yelled and spit inadvertently in the inmate's face, calling him all kinds of names. I remember thinking that I had never seen a white man talk to another white man like that before. I was to learn over the course of my stay in jail that being locked up ironically offered us more equality than being on the outside. Not justice, but equality. In the world, the governing bodies make rules, and beneath them the privileged are afforded the choice to adhere or disobey, depending on their status. The social hierarchy continues down in levels, each group who sits above another exerting their power and influence over them. Special treatment is doled out in various forms. And if you know the right people, or have the right kind of money, you can subvert any system.

Not in jail. In confinement, there are only two populations: you and them. The "you" does not consist of particular racial groups, social statuses, or demographics, as it does on the outside. Everybody who wears an orange jump suit (or the classic black and white chain gang get-up if you're especially lucky) is your group. You will be oppressed. You will be harmed. Degraded, disrespected, and disregarded. *White, black, rich, or poor. No love in Atlantis 4.* That's what they said in there. I found the dynamic quite interesting, paradoxically uplifting. I figured if I had to choose a side, I'd much rather pick the one with Dog on it.

When we finally got to the caf, Dakota and I went through the line behind Worm, Darren, and OJ. All of the food looked like puree. We've all heard the jokes about prison food, but my stomach turned at the sight of it. I know jail is supposed to be a punishment, but the food looked so bad, I was certain the cooks had to be making it disgusting on purpose. Dakota had some of the mystery puree spooned onto his tray along with a hunk of blonde cornbread. I opted for the cereal and grabbed the cornbread just for kicks.

We sat down with Worm, Darren, and OJ. Nobody talked much. I lifted a spoonful of cereal into my mouth and nearly choked from the taste. The cereal itself was tart—a stronger taste than being just stale. The milk was filmy and weird-tasting too. At the same time, Dakota had taken a bite of the cornbread and was subsequently scraping it off of his tongue with a napkin.

"This cereal...It's stale," I complained.

"Really?" said OJ, "Lemme taste."

OJ took a huge gulp of the cereal. He swished it around in his mouth and then swallowed, smacking his lips.

"Nah. That tastes about normal."

My jaw dropped. OJ continued eating his meal, unfazed. I turned to look at Dakota, whose mouth was also agape, his cornbread littered tongue hanging. I started to laugh. At first it was somewhat of a chuckle at how silly Dakota looked. But then I started thinking about how ridiculous our entire situation was. I thought about the food, our fellow inmates, our interactions with the cops—and how funny it would be once it was all over. My chuckle evolved into a strong laugh, and I noticed that Dakota was laughing with me. Hearing Dakota's laugh made me laugh even harder. He used to laugh very hard for three or four seconds and then wheeze deeply before starting again. Within a couple minutes, we were both laughing hysterically. I'm sure the other inmates must have thought we were crazy.

But I think that was the second important lesson I learned in jail; you have to cope.

The sad truth is that to survive, you have to desensitize yourself to the inhumane treatment. In the outside world, it's hard to justify this desensitization because we have the illusion of true freedom, although we are bound by many more circumstances than we perceive. The terrible food didn't elicit a response from OJ because he was used to it. Nobody told the crying inmate to be quiet because they empathized. Powerless in reality, the only method of maintaining your sanity was finding strength in something. You had to cope. Our strength was in our understanding of the world, and the way that it should be. We had the upper hand because the worse we were treated, in our minds, the farther from an acceptable reality we drifted. Quickly drifting from verisimilitude off-course to an isle of farce, why would we take anything seriously? A flawed theory, perhaps, but coping mechanisms only have to make sense to those healing. The laughter was our medicine.

The next twenty-four hours was a blur. We adapted surprisingly quickly to the culture of the jail. Dakota chatted with the inmates. I learned a lot through observation. We ate more awful food, but most of all, we slept. Dakota still wasn't talking to me much, but I didn't mind. I figured any of my other friends I had put in this predicament would probably berate me to no end. He was a real class act, Dakota was. He just kind of kept quiet and went through the motions. At times he was so comfortable in the jail, it was eerie. Those glimpses of assimilation made me think about how easy it must be to become institutionalized. Perseverance in any sense requires understanding the reality of your situation and then making the most of your resources to overcome it. If your situation is forty years in jail, then it's less about overcoming and more about sustaining. Here we were, two kids barely out of our teens, coming to terms with a fate that, days prior, we had never imagined was in the realm of possibility for our lives. I thought about Dog and Darren and others. What reason did they really have to prioritize anything higher than "getting by?" Survival was the name of the game. I think we probably learned more about survival in those few days than most of our friends had learned up until that point in their lives.

We did learn about one major thing on Thursday: lockdown. During the daylight hours, we had a big block of time to move about from the cell to the recreation room, or maybe outside to play sports or lift weights. This was unless, of course, a correctional officer shift change overlapped with our recreation time that day. If that was the case, then all inmates would have to migrate back to their cells and be locked in until the shift change was completed. I'm not sure exactly how it was orchestrated, but it took forever. We were locked down for four hours that Thursday and ended up missing the last hour or so of our free time. I was so confused because there didn't appear to be so many C.O.s that it should take that long. Dakota and I slept most of the time we were locked down. When we woke up, we had another date in the world's greatest cafeteria, I avoided another shower, and we went back to our cells for the night.

Midway through the third or fourth iteration of my push-up workout, Dakota called out to me. I had thought he was asleep.

"You know...while you were arguing with that cop...couple days ago? The other cop was asking me...like telling me that if I would just tell him what *really* happened, then he would let me go...I think he wanted to me to you know...just put it all on you."

"And you didn't do it?"

"Of course not."

"I'm sorry Dakota. I'm really sorry, man. But, thank you. Really don't know where I'd be without you."

"It's cool, man."

I heard him turn over in the dark. He was asleep soon after our conversation, and I paused my push-ups for a while. Dakota had always felt like I was to blame in the situation, and rightly so. He thought I didn't realize just how many hits he had taken for me. I figured that was why he had been so quiet. After my apology, things started becoming normal between us again. He just wanted me to understand that he was there for me, no matter what. Nobody ever had to pull an apology out of me again after that day, ever. Dakota made me a better friend. I'll be forever thankful to him for that.

We woke up the next morning to the clinking of cardboard on our cell bars. One of the C.O.s was rapping on the bars to wake us up.

"Abrams, Zola?"

"Yeah."

"You'll see the judge this morning; be ready in twenty."

I felt all the feeling go out of my body, like I was floating. I was so excited. Dakota and I talked about all the things we would do once we got out until the guard came back to get us. The one thing we were both most excited about was the food. We couldn't wait to eat. We dreamed up the most delicious meals and made ourselves even hungrier talking about them. They sat us in a small waiting room with too many other inmates, but we didn't mind so much. We figured there was no way the judge would actually hold us. I wasn't quite as naïve as I was when I had first entered the jail, but talks with the inmates had assured me that there was no case against us. They called Dakota first, of course. Abrams. He passed through a door into a different room on the other side of the waiting room we were in. I was jealous and excited at the same time.

I had been so wrapped up in carrying on conversations with the other freedom-awaiting inmates that I didn't realize how much time was passing. I spent an hour, two hours, three hours in the waiting room, watching as the pool of inmates grew smaller and smaller. With the last name Zola, I assumed I was last, but when there were about four of us left in the room, I began to get nervous. What if we ran out of time? What if I didn't get called? How would I ever connect back with Dakota? I hadn't thought of any of these things when they called us into the room, but in the moment, I remembered Mikey saying that if the judge couldn't see us on Friday, then he would see us Monday. I felt like I was going to throw up. The thought of spending two more days in jail after being so close to freedom was paralyzing. I was the last one in the room at this point. I waited minutes that felt like lifetimes. Finally, the C.O. came back into the room. I stood up anxiously.

"Come on."

I started to walk toward the door I had seen everyone else walking through and was met with a firm hand in the chest.

"Other way."

"What? I'm not getting out? What's going on?"

You guessed it.

Lockdown.

Processing the other inmates out had taken so long that the next shift change had occurred. Now we would be on lockdown for another God knows how long, and there was a very real possibility that I could remain in jail over the weekend. I slouched back to my cell and tried to hold back the tears. I saw OJ on the way back. He didn't say anything but gave me a look of sympathy. All those guys were rooting for us. Dejection is an understatement. I didn't even have enough motivation to do push-ups. I lay on the bed feeling like a zombie. I passively watched the sun complete its slow fall toward the horizon. I only shed a couple of tears. I was too exhausted to cry. When lockdown ended, they took us to dinner. I was starving. I ate all the mush and slush they had, including (supposed) wheat versions of the cornbread we had grown to uh...know and love, if you will. They called the wheat ones brownies. The food gave me enough energy to do push-ups, so I decided when I got back to the cell I would tire myself out and try to go to sleep early. The more of the next couple days I could pass by sleeping, the better. When I got back to my cell, a C.O. was standing outside the door.

"You ready?"

I hesitated to answer because I wasn't quite sure what he meant.

"Out processing. You ready to leave? The judge is waiting."

I followed the C.O. back to the same room as earlier, more confused than I've ever been. Had the judge sat in that other room for the entire day? The roller-coaster day had taken a toll on me mentally. I couldn't even be excited immediately that I didn't have to spend the time in jail I thought I did. I was just trying to make sense of everything.

The C.O. took me into the room and through the glorious door I had waited so long to pass through. The room on the other side was reminiscent of a confessional booth. There was a small stool seated in front of a screen that was seated in the wall. I chose to stand. After a few seconds, the screen flickered on, and I saw the judge. He was a professionally dressed, middle-aged white man with the remainder of his rust-colored hair gelled backward and small circular glasses sitting at the end of his nose. This felt like the Wizard of Oz. This was what we had been waiting for? A man on a screen? We could have seen the judge literally any time from the moment we were booked! All he had to do was turn on a camera. I grew hot with anger. I was mad at the stupidity of the system and even more mad that I had no control over it. I tried to keep my cool, though. I didn't want to do or say anything that would jeopardize my freedom.

The judge and I went through some formal, preliminary questions: who I was, what I was charged with, date and time, etc. I thought the entire process would be like that, but since Dakota had already been processed and released, the judge made quick work of the entire thing. I don't really remember the particulars, but it ended with:

"You are free to go. Please follow the direction of the correctional officer outside the room."

I changed back into my regular clothes in another small room and was led down a hallway to a metal corridor. At the end of the corridor was a heavy, bolted door with a small window in it. The sunlight was soft, peeking from behind the hills. As the door closed behind me, I looked ahead to see Dakota, his father, my father, my girlfriend, and the rest of our friends. I walked down the path to them and up to my dad first. He gave me a look that said, *I don't know how you got yourself into such a mess or how you're going to explain it, but I'm relieved to see you.* We hugged for a while before I hugged and talked to everybody there. My girlfriend had spent her last money taking a cab all the way to the jail. She had also called all of my friends and my parents once they had realized what happened to me, trying to get a hold of anyone who could help.

I never even thought about cheating on her again.

Our friends tried hard to find us Wednesday night, to no avail. Thursday morning they were talking to some locals who suggested they try the local jails. They mentioned that during spring break season, the city hires mercenary cops to come into the area for more protection. They had checked the websites of a few of the largest local jails for recent arrests and found us, sure enough. Around the same time, Salvador had called both my father and Dakota's father and told him our stories. They said he was very poised and eloquent on the phone, mentioning that we seemed like good boys, and he hoped we would be okay. Our fathers flew in separately and carpooled to the jail together Friday morning in anticipation of our release. Whenever it comes to mind, I say a prayer for Salvador.

"You boys wanna get something to eat?" asked Dakota's father as we headed toward the rental car.

Dakota nudged me and smiled. "I waited for you," he said.

I didn't tell him right away that I had gotten so full off the crap in jail that I couldn't possibly eat another thing. We went to a buffet, and I sat back and smiled as he devoured the food, continuing to ask me, "you sure you don't want something?" with a full mouth. All I could do was smile. He really was a great friend.

The crazy finale isn't so crazy. Technically, we had two more days of spring break left before we had to head back to school.

Our fathers left in the morning, and since it was the weekend, my friends were preparing for the next spring break crowd to be arriving. It was guaranteed to be a ton of fun on the beach Saturday and Sunday with the kids who were starting their spring break, as well as those of us who were finishing ours. Dakota snapped back to reality pretty quickly. A true pragmatist, he was going to make the most out of his remaining break. I slept mostly all day Saturday and Sunday. I spent some time with my girlfriend, but mainly I slept. Before my sleep marathon though, I woke up at about five a.m. Saturday morning. I hadn't really slept well during the night, and after an hour or so of sitting in the darkness, I decided to take a walk. I walked down the pier toward the strip. I stopped for a moment outside the club where we had been arrested. It looked shabby in the morning light, dry and lifeless. I took off my shoes and walked toward the beach through the sand. It was cool between my toes, not like during the day when getting to the water felt like punishment. I sat on the shore and listened to the waves. I watched the sunrise and the sky change color with the coming of a new day. Breathing in the salty air was refreshing—it hadn't been before. I dug my toes into the sand, and stretched my arms out to let the strong breezes blow through me when they came. I enjoyed every single part of being free. I promised myself never to forget what it felt like to be on the beach that morning. And I never did.

***

The audience and Mack Morristerr had been amazed the entire time Dr. Zola recounted his story. The segment that had begun as a deep dive into the makeup of a feature film had transformed into an emotional roller-coaster of a tribute to the late, great Dakota Abrams. Everyone could finally understand why this mysterious doctor had been chosen to advise on a movie like *Distinction*, which was so filled with introspection of the human condition and lessons to live by. During the segment, Dr. Zola had been almost in a trance, abandoning his usual meek, soft-spoken nature and displaying all the skills of a seasoned and impassioned chronicler-orator. Now that his story had finished, he seemed once again conscious of his environment and anxiously wiped his brow in anticipation of the segment's end.

"Wow. What a tale. I don't think there's any more questions as to why you were chosen to support the project after Mr. Abrams passed. I truly believe that he is smiling down on what you were able to help create in his absence," Mack Morristerr mused.

The comment made Dr. Zola tear up a bit. He hadn't really thought deeply about Dakota since the funeral. The image of an ethereal Dakota, resplendent and satisfied with Dr. Zola was almost too powerful for his friend to bear.

"I'll say this...as a last thing," Dr. Zola said, trying to keep from choking up. "As I sat on that beach that Saturday morning, I thought about the son I hoped to have one day...the son I have now. Elijah. And I always thought..."

The tears began to flow freely.

"...I always thought, *When I tell him this story, it's going to teach him that it's okay not to be a hero. You don't have to feel bad that you're not the one to save the day. That we're just regular people, and you shouldn't feel ashamed if you can't change the world.* I thought like that because a part of me always regretted picking up that phone. But after telling this story today, I realize something that I've never thought about. Dakota was a hero that week and every day of his life. I know he's a hero to many of you here now. And so I think...I think when I tell my son this story, I'm going to tell him what it takes to change the world. I'm going to explain to him what it takes to be a hero, because I believe he can be extraordinary. I might be ordinary, and I'm okay with that. But my son is special, like his Uncle Dakota. And there's nobody I'd rather him aspire to be like. Every day that he wakes up, I want him to feel how I felt on the beach that Saturday. Every day. And at the end of his life, he's going to know that those who loved him wouldn't have made it without him. That he was their breeze on the shore. Their candle in the dark. Their peace amidst the storm. That he was their hero. And I can only teach him because Dakota taught me. And I can never pay Dakota back for that. But I hope he knows I'm thankful...I'm so thankful."

Dr. Zola wiped his eyes. The applause that the crowd had burst into was nothing more than muffled droning in his ears. He stood up and shook hands with Mack Morristerr, who complemented the formality with a half-hug. Dr. Zola waved to the crowd and exited stage left into the backstage area. Elijah was on his mind. He thought of Dakota as he wiped the tear trails from his cheeks with his shirt cuffs. He stepped outside the studio into the parking lot and let the cool, night air wash over him. The stars were bright in the violet sky. They were a bit brighter than he remembered. He let the starlight illuminate his path home, taking the backroads with the windows down all the way.

Real Monsters

Much Madness is divinest Sense -
To a discerning Eye -
Much Sense - the starkest Madness -
'Tis the Majority
In this, as all, prevail -
Assent - and you are sane -
Demur - you're straightway dangerous -
And handled with a Chain -
Emily Dickinson

There are those who believe in the Sight: seers, soothsayers, and savants. The paragons of this group possess the abilities of Sight themselves. Then, there are those who believe in the power of the third eye, but try as they might, they cannot channel their energy to view the world through it. Over time, the allure of perception beyond visual sight fades, and the shades of gray in the world hum a mellowing tune, goading you to clear your mind of your farfetched illusions of vibrancy.

Most important (because the majority is always most important) are those who fail to both acknowledge and recognize the power of the Sight and Seers. The world is to them only as it appears to be. The sun goes up in the morning and comes down at dusk. The rules are meant to be followed. We live to die. That is the way it is. These are the people who keep the world spinning comfortably on its axis. Their condition is catching, and with all the presence of mind of a seasoned zombie, they meander through this life, their brains producing a low, buzzing drone, only aroused and alarmed by the presence of difference. A dissenter in their midst means one more taste of sweet, true life before it's back to the low, buzzing drone, and the taste of life is nothing more than a blurry memory.

All throughout history there are accounts of the dual-eyed zombies conquering the nonpareils. The Maid of Orleans cried out to her savior as she was burned for heresy. El-Hajj Malik El-Shabazz had "too much power." God's son walked on water, and they called him a liar. We love fairy tales because the hero always wins and good prevails. This affinity is nothing more than a pitiful reaching grasp for circumstances that we are conditioned to believe are not ideal, but expected. Yet in reality, we experience a much different dynamic. Still, the glass remains half-full. We shed tears for the jilted lover and the defeated champion. It is the same reason Margaret wept over Goldengrove. We want to believe that justice is orthodox. This hopeful yearning is what makes humans beautifully unique, which I suppose is justification enough for such an ill-advised philosophy. *C'est la vie.*

But for now, on to our story.

***

The building was a mass of pale concrete, stories high amongst an otherwise vibrant strip of downtown shops and stores. It appeared as if the sidewalk had decided to grow upward one day, and fed by the abundance of food and drink dropped and spilled daily by pedestrians, mutated into a monster of a building, head and shoulders over everything else in the area. It was so much so an aberration within the landscape that passersby often stopped while passing it, checked their maps, or spun around confusedly to get their bearings. For they imagined there was no way a building of this sort should be on the path to their destination in the downtown arts district. If they had happened to pass this gray gargantuan, they must have gone too far. Alas, many of these people soon discovered that the eyesore that had shaken them from their walking daydream was the very same building they had been seeking. Etched on a small, tarnished gold plate right above the doorway sat an understated statement of purpose: *Research.*

Laypersons could earn up to one hundred dollars in two hours for completing any of the various tasks affiliated with marketing research. Sometimes they filled out surveys. Other times they sat in focus groups. Often times, participants would arrive and be told that they were no longer needed for the study, receiving fifty dollars for their trouble of travel. Those in-the-know looked forward to this latter scenario.

On this night, four participants—the only four who had been chosen—traveled to the research building, all arriving within twenty minutes of each other. They each checked in at the front desk and made their way through the turnstile to the elevators down the hall, on the left, as the concierge had instructed. Each traveled up to the third floor and passed through a beige door into a small corridor. The first of three red doors on the right side of the corridor led to a small waiting room, which each of them eventually found. They waited, sipping water and scrolling through their phones while the facilitator prepared the focus group room.

"I'll periodically come in to check with you all and see if you want to ask any questions of the participants in addition to what I have already slated to ask them. Sound good?" asked the facilitator to the clients.

After receiving a nod of approval, she exited the observation room—a rectangular room, dimly lit on the darkened side of a one-way mirror. Vedon let out a grunt of anticipatory glee. Haadis yawned and tugged at the bottom of her mask, the part around the collarbone, and watched as the observers settled in. The mask fit poorly, and exposed the pale, purple, pachyderm skin, true to most creatures of her kind. The facilitator took her place at the head of the table in the focus group room, and used her walkie-talkie to alert her assistant to send the participants in.

The participants filed in one-by-one and sat at the gray, rectangular, resin tables. There were three tables arranged in a U-shape, at the base of which sat Marjorie, the facilitator. The tables featured various scratches and scrapes from years of use. In the summer, the research building hired high school kids to work as custodial staff for the public-access portions of the building. This served the purposes of keeping otherwise subject-to-troublemaking youth busy and putting money in their pockets, as well as making the profane sharpie tattoos on tables, chairs, and other furniture less visible, and normally lemon-scented.

Each participant was equipped with a freshly sharpened No. 2 pencil as well as one sheet of college-ruled, loose-leaf paper. Their chairs were the gray-beige folding steel chairs that many churches use for their events.

"Hello, and welcome," began Marjorie. "Today you will participate in a focus group about consumer advertising. My name is Marjorie, and I'll be your facilitator. Even though I'll be asking you many questions, I want this to be a discussion. Do not be afraid to speak your mind. If you have an opinion that conflicts with the opinion of someone in the room, please don't be shy. This works best when everybody says exactly how they feel."

The participants stared blankly at Marjorie.

"So...we'll be here for about two hours. Before I get started asking questions, why don't we go around, and everybody can say who they are, where they're from, and what they do?"

"Well, my name is Dal, and I'm from India...but I have been working here for about ten years. I am a nurse at the Memorial Hospital right up the street. I have a wife, Indira, and three kids, and we live east of the city, across the water."

"Thank you, Dal," chimed Marjorie. Dal looked down at his shoes and wrung his steadily perspiring hands.

The next to speak was Cecily, the late twenty-something, self-proclaimed "cool girl." An aspiring model and singer, she and her Bohemian crew of flunkies were completely ensnared by all things "retro." They lived for glass Coca-Cola bottles, faded overalls, and cult classic movies. Their zealous obsession with the look and feel of the world prompted them to schedule and pay for professional photo shoots an average of once every three months. Afterward, they would look through the pictures and post their favorites to social media. They never did anything else with them. Shallow as Cecily may have seemed, however, she was much sharper than she let on.

Sade Diggory was third, a meek woman who had been so nervous racking her brain about what to say for her introduction, she hadn't realized everyone else was only giving their first names, and so she introduced herself in the way she was taught was most appropriate. She was a pretty, middle-aged woman, but her beauty was hidden beneath a frumpy shell of low self-esteem.

She had not always been this way. Once upon a time, Sade Diggory was a sunflower in a lily field: different and lovely and special all in her own right. She was a free-thinker and an artist, spending most of her days on the sunporch her parents had built for her such that on bright days, just the right amount of light beamed through the space to inspire the passions of a creator. She was skilled with a paintbrush, brilliant with various instruments, and especially spirited with verse. Unfortunately, she did not take to people (or them to her) quite as well as she took to the arts. Her youth was a muddled puddle of confusion, socially. By college she felt that she had missed her prime opportunity for the acculturation and assimilation that makes most young people able to acquire friends. Her passion for art faded; she no longer wanted to create isolated instances of beauty. She would gladly trade her skill (if the lonely dorm room nights went with it) to feel that she was a part of something. And so the sunflower began its transformation into a lily. The process was tedious, yet effective. By the end, the melodic tones that had once escaped the mouth of the lark that was Sade had devolved to rather shrill tones, screeched from high above. Though in unison with those of her newfound brethren, the screeches garnered as much favor with Sade as an angel's harp.

"Um, hi. I'm Aislyn. Well, Lyn. I'm from the neighborhood. I, um. Well, I was in school and then I stopped for a while. Didn't really see the point you know? Felt that I could probably self-teach, or even invest the money I was busting my ass to pay tuition with into something with a more immediate, profitable return. But, I don't know. The winds of life kinda blew me back into the classroom, and so I'm coming up on my last semester this fall. I like music, sports, books...I like to read about different stuff, you know? Like aliens. I just started this book about Area 51 and Roswell. I started reading about government conspiracies and aliens maybe a year or so ago. I'm pretty sure there's something else out there, you know? I feel like there's much more to this world than we see at first glance. We owe it to ourselves to double-take."

Cecily took a loud sip of water from the smudged glass cup in front of her.

"Okay, then," said Marjorie.

The clock on the wall ticked loudly with the passing of each second.

"Well, I'm going to get started. I'm guessing you all are aware at this point that today we'll be talking about food advertising. So, who can name a couple of the popular food chains here in town?" asked Marjorie.

"Patty's Melts," called out Dal, a little too quickly. "I um, always eat that on my break. There's one right by the hospital."

In the adjacent room, Marjorie's assistant smacked loudly on a chicken melt from Patty's.

Beebo's. Brightside Cafe. McArnold's. Captain Kidd's Fishhouse. Knuckles Drive-In. The crew rattled off many names quickly. The city was fast, and required fast-food for fast people living fast lives.

After a brief silence, Marjorie asked the group if they had any more chains they would like to have added to the list. Following another brief silence, she asked if they had ever heard of The Beach Apple.

"Oh, yeah! That's like, the healthy place, right? Lots of different salads. And they have a hammock in the store. Way cool. But I heard there's a lot of bad stuff in the food though. That the ingredients aren't very healthy," chimed Sade.

"Oh my god, they have the best burrito bowls," added Cecily.

"Yes, I know this place very well," said Dal. "My wife prefers me to bring this home for the kids. Because it is fast food, but yet not really fast food, right? More of a...healthy fast food."

Marjorie scribbled furiously on the board, taking notes about everything the participants had to say about The Beach Apple restaurant.

Vedon and Haadis grinned behind the glass as their associates scribbled their own notes about the particulars of the participants' remarks.

"Yeah. So to my knowledge, that place really *isn't* all that healthy, right? I mean, they claim that all their ingredients are 'fresh' and 'natural,' but hardly ever specify what that means. I think I heard that some of their meats and vegetables are genetically modified."

It was Lyn.

The room grew quiet. Marjorie inadvertently looked backward toward the dark side of the glass before catching herself and facing forward once more. The associates of Vedon and Haadis stopped scribbling. The two lead monsters themselves grew still.

"Say more," goaded Marjorie.

"I think it was the chicken. The chickens aren't free range, or raised on a vegetarian diet, or any of that stuff we hear that's supposed to be better, more humane, healthier. They use the genetically enhanced animals, the ones whose growth is manipulated because the end goal is for them to be eaten, so they're pumped full of all types of hormones and stuff. Same with the vegetables, sprayed with all kinds of pesticides and preservatives. Frozen and shipped, not locally grown. I mean, I feel like it's pretty much what all of these places do, but The Beach Apple is...I don't know...almost lying in a way by insinuating that they're different from everyone else."

"To me, the fact that they're serving menu items—salads, sandwiches, soups, wraps—that are much healthier than burgers, fries, shit like that...definitely makes them a healthier option," contested Cecily.

"Not if the ingredients in those things aren't healthy at all," mumbled Lyn.

"Really?" snapped Cecily, as loud as Lyn should have been. "So an 'unhealthy' salad is worse than an unhealthy burger? You sound stupid."

"Let's not get disrespectful," said Marjorie the mediator. "These are good points. Let's move on to an advertisement I'd like to share with you all."

She dimmed the lights and turned the screen on to show the commercial. It was a rather cheesy commercial, depicting a mix among young, hip teenagers and classic American families enjoying the fare of The Beach Apple. A reimagining of a current Top 40 pop song played in the background. The actors laughed and smiled while they sat and enjoyed their meals. At the end, the father in the family had a sudden realization that caused him to check his watch urgently. His whole family froze in anticipation. After noticing the time, the father shrugged off his prior urgency and reclined once more in his booth to enjoy the rest of his food with a smile, prompting his family into a shared *"that was close"* type of chuckle. In the final frame, the family walked out of the restaurant and into the parking lot arm in arm. As the sun set and the screen darkened, the phrase, *Marvelous food, fast,* was super-imposed on the screen.

As the lights awakened in the room, Marjorie asked, "So, what do we think about that commercial? How does it make us feel about The Beach Apple?"

Dal was the first to respond.

"You see, it's good, this commercial. I like it because it shows how tough balance is for a family, for a father in a family. I get The Beach Apple for my little ones often, because my hours at the hospital make it hard to cook, and Indira has many things to do. I feel guilty that...that I don't always cook for my children. That I don't give them this nutritious things, right? But The Beach Apple is the best option if I cannot cook, because it's more healthy than other foods that are just as fast."

Lyn turned away from the table, impudent, mumbling "It's not even healthier..."

"I think it was great!" piped Sade, beaming.

"It was cute, or whatever. Sweet, I guess. The whole perfect family thing. I can see how most people would like it," said Cecily.

"But you didn't like it? It didn't make you feel anything?" asked Marjorie.

"It was completely cheesy, honestly."

"Well, I thought it was sort of sweet...but I can see what you mean, Cecily...very...cliché?" said Sade backpedaling.

"Sade, don't let Cecily change your mind. If you thought it was sweet, it was sweet. It's supposed to speak to people like you: middle-aged, family folks," contested Lyn.

"Well, I uh...I don't really have a family," said Sade, ashamed.

And of course, the subsequent awkward silence one would expect in this scenario.

"Look, Lyn. Don't be upset because I have my own ideas. The commercial was meant to target a certain group of people. I think it did that effectively, however corny it may have been. You should listen more to the actual question and stop putting so much emphasis on the nutritional facts, which aren't even up for discussion here," said Cecily.

"Well it's kind of hard for me to take anyone seriously who can watch that commercial and 'get it,' when everything is a lie. If their product isn't what they say it is, then everything we see— the family having fun, the joy, the health—it's all a lie. None of it is real," responded Lyn.

"Really? Because the last time I checked, perception was pretty closely tied to an individual's reality," said Cecily, sarcastically. "Your mind state is that elevated, huh? That you get your kicks by infiltrating the realities of unknowing strangers and making them question every single thing they've ever known to be true? Have you ever been happy? Ignorance is a bliss like none other. Not everything needs an explanation. Things are supposed to work, and so they do. The commercial was supposed to evoke an emotional response that would prompt consumers to support the product based on a sense of aligned values. If people get that, and they're happy, are you the hero or the villain for keeping them from it?"

The room was tense. Lyn had never thought about things this way. Everybody should want to know the truth; everybody should always have the right answer. And if they didn't, it was your job to give it to them. Lyn had always considered deconstructing false realities a hero's work, and knowing that the truth hurts, had taken the reactions of those newly liberated (however strong) to be natural for folks whose eyes had just been opened for the first time. Having encountered anger, aggression, and hurt from various parties, Lyn now had to consider that the origin of these feelings was a place of fear, confusion, and perhaps even depression caused by a kid who felt a little too strongly about one too many things. It was a hard pill to swallow.

"Great discussion. Let's move along," said Marjorie.

The group continued to discuss. Lyn continued to brood. They viewed several other advertisements in various forms. There were commercials, online ads, web page schematics, mobile advertisements, and then some early draft concepts of television advertising to come. The Beach Apple was promoted as a healthy, family-friendly restaurant that could provide you with a quick, nutritious alternative to the common fast-food places at which most folks have been scared out of eating. The truth was that L-cysteine, wood pulp, sodium nitrite, sand, Dimethylpolysiloxane, and MSM were as frequent in the breads and meats offered at The Beach Apple as any other chain. The manager at the location close to the research facility sometimes brought vegetables in from the local farmer's market if the corporate shipment was behind or if some vegetables were especially cheap that day. But this was against protocol, as these foods had not been inspected and cleared (the irony) through the supply chain process.

Furthermore, it wasn't a dedication to health and wellness or a desire to affect change that drove the manager to purchase local items for use in the store. He always grabbed a few things for the house on the days that the farmer's market was set up blocks away from his apartment. He normally brought too many things home, at which point his wife would exclaim, "What am I gonna do with all of this? You're just bringing food in here to spoil!" So, after a while, he started buying extra on purpose. He'd let his wife take the choice items, and he'd bring the rest in to work. Apart from the manager's second-tier market vegetables, the other ingredients in The Beach Apple store in the city and nationwide were marinated in pesticides and drizzled with preservatives long before they ever reached a customer's palate.

Vedon and Haadis stood behind the glass in the darkened room mumbling to each other in the low, grumbling tones of their native language. To the untrained ear, it sounded like throaty gurgling, a choking of sorts. They ceased talking when a ray of light crept into the group from the hallway. It was Marjorie. Haadis adjusted her mask slyly.

"Hi. Um. Is everything going okay? Is there anything in particular you'd like me to ask? I only have a few more exercises to take them through."

"The dissenter. Ask what kind of actions could be taken to...change their views on our restaurant," said Vedon. Even though he always spoke first, it was clear if you were in a room with the two of them that Haadis was the one in charge.

"Well, I would have to figure out a way to frame it to the whole group so it didn't seem as if I was singling Lyn out."

"Which is your job, is it not?" said Haadis. Her voice was level and calm, but very sharp. When she spoke, it made you unsure of yourself.

Marjorie hurried from the room and closed the door. Vedon, Haadis, and the rest of the monsters chuckled at her silly human ways. Haadis removed her right claw from her pocket and motioned for one of the associates to lock the door to the observation room. When it was locked, she removed her mask first, then Vedon, then the rest of the associates, per protocol. Their masks temporarily disposed of, purple flesh exposed, the monsters took what we would call a break. Vedon pulled a bag of carrots out from the cabinet and passed them around the group. The monsters' diet consisted of ninety percent vegetables. Certain populations had developed a taste for leavened bread as they had become more familiar with human societies, the most gluttonous even indulging in a muffin or pastry every once in a blue moon. The creatures are well built, some slender, some bulkier, but all very lean and strong. The males and females are almost identical, save for the fact that the females are decidedly larger in stature. Their faces are flat, their features rigid, somewhat like reptiles. Not much of a nose is augmented with two air holes for sensory intake. They had used this function while still in the wild to forage for food and to remain aware of their surroundings. They actually breathe through gills in their necks that strip Earth's air of its oxygen and leave primarily nitrogen, which is essential to their respiratory process. Oxygen is not poisonous to them, but they breathe easier without it.

Their eyes had started out similar to those of owls, but over time, with increased exposure to light, had become close enough to human eyes not to require much cosmetic effort to keep a low profile in the presence of humans. Their teeth are many and square, ideal for crushing the various types of vegetables they liked to eat. From the center of the forehead, up and across the top of the cranium, down the neck and back was a row of hardened flesh, scales if you will, that adorned each creature. These scales are the only distinct feature for many of the monsters. Some shine like holograms, and it was most difficult to find any two monsters with the same color, shape, and orientation of scales. The appearance varied even within families. They have no ears, but instead hollow, grooved holes in their necks which allowed them to "hear" through sonar. Long limbs end in "hands" and "feet," each with slender phalanges that harden and sharpen with every inch closer to its terminal. These odd hands make it uncomfortable to wear human gloves, and with such big hands, the monsters were limited in their options of being discreet. Haadis often chose to forego the use of gloves, instead relying on deep pockets, informal gatherings, and dim lighting to keep her cover.

The bag of carrots diminished; each monster pulled its mask back on. The focus group was coming to a close, but they had heard enough. They were in good shape; no fear of their cover being blown any time soon. There was always one dissenter, but they never prevailed above the group. The monsters thought it was funny that humans treated others with unique ideas and perspectives so rashly. Haadis herself had rose to power with the very cavalier plan that the monster population was enacting currently; the reason they were holding focus groups. Every so often, a human would see through the admittedly thin veneer of respectability that the monsters had built for The Beach Apple. In the beginning, it scared them. They considered making various changes to make the plan more foolproof. The original idea had indeed been undercooked, but it had come down to theory vs. action at a very crucial time, and Haadis decided to launch the project early. As the concept testing continued, however, and the monsters noticed how humans treated the demurrers, it almost became a source of amusement. Arrogant, perhaps, but Vedon and most other associates were thoroughly entertained that humans could so easily ignore the truth right in front of their very eyes. The added bonus of them persecuting people who sought to open their eyes to the truth was nearly too much hilarity to endure.

Haadis was more cautious of the dissenters and their potential. She had, after all, been a dissenter in her own right.

Their race had watched over a span of nearly three-hundred years as humans deforested many lands all over the world and created unnecessary and unproductive structures. This race of monsters was not inherently violent, and had been totally okay with cohabiting with humans, as long as the two groups retained the proper separation. With the forests, their homes, dwindling, the monsters had a choice to make: reveal themselves to humans and seek to live in harmony, or derive a plan to continue to live and thrive in secrecy. Haadis had proposed a veil that the monsters could live under, just temporarily, until they found a part of the Earth that was less developed, and once they were sure that that place was safe and secure, they would relocate there. Her younger brother Vedon had been one of only a few who supported her plan. The leadership of their tribe was not among that few. In a fantastic presentation one fall, the elder monsters (who had had more time to develop human language) exited what was left of the forest and made contact with humans.

It was fair and carnival season. Most of the humans in the town right outside the forest were enjoying the festivities of the traveling fair: rides, food delicacies, games, and other fare of the season. But especially the food. The humans gorged on turkey legs and funnel cakes, many things fried and others placed on sticks. They took great joy in these food items, as judged by the gleeful expressions of humans young and old with each bite taken. The monsters had chosen to expose themselves at the fair so that they could be seen and confirmed by a mass of the population. Through their observation, that knew that humans were skeptical, fanciful creatures, very given to imaginative thinking and farfetched stories. The monsters wanted to make it as clear as possible what they were and why they were emerging from the remains of the forest. Unfortunately, the plan was a complete disaster. These humans being country folks, and the monsters being unarmed, a massive slaughter of Haadis's race occurred that day, thereafter forever known to the monsters as The Plight of Iresine. Axes and hatchets came swiftly down upon the unprepared race, who, although physically superior, were in the end undone by their naïve and trusting nature. Bullets littered the air as the monsters retreated back into the forest. Only a few made it far enough into the trees to escape the barrage. These monsters do not shed tears, as humans do, but go through bouts of silence to express their sadness and mourning. Four days of silence passed deep in the woods before any monster spoke up. When one finally did, it was Ceri.

He charged the monsters to strike back. To use their superior physical strength and mental abilities to obliterate the townspeople. His speech was so impassioned that many of the monsters were riled up and began to dream of a mighty rally with which they could overtake the humans. But Vedon, a younger and smaller male than Ceri, rushed him as he spoke, tackling him to the ground. He struck Ceri repeatedly about the face and neck, knocking him into a disoriented state. "Is this what you want?!?" he growled. "More violence? More pain? More bloodshed?" He continued to strike Ceri until two of the older males pulled him away. He shook loose of their grip and addressed the group.

"We had a plan. We had a way to do this in secret, as we always have. We are not a violent race. We have always been content with just our share, even if we had to ration it by the light of the moon. With the blood of many of our brothers and sisters staining the ground...what has changed about that?"

The crowd was silent. They knew that they had lost their composure in light of the massacre, but Vedon was right. They should take an approach that could guarantee the safety of their kind. For if only one objective was achieved, they would need it to be safety. Vedon had just become the champion male by defeating Ceri in a physical contest. Everyone would follow his lead now. With their attention captured, he motioned for Haadis to face the crowd and address her people.

"I have an idea."

It was all very simple. First, the monsters would create disguises. They couldn't risk being recognized and persecuted again. Those who were most familiar with humans agreed that they could design pieces of clothing that resembled human characteristics, for what better place to hide than in plain sight? With these disguises, the monsters would assimilate into human culture, but not completely, and not directly. It would require years of tactful planning and execution. Some humans might have to die, so the monsters could assume their identities. Ultimately, Haadis wanted to design a systematic way to gain control over the humans. Her initial thought was to steer them away from their own destructive habits once in control of them, but as she and her family mourned, and years continued to pass of watching the destruction of Earth intensify, they began to feel as if the humans were getting exactly what they bargained for. After a few years of lying low and assuming the identities of prominent humans in large cities within the region, Haadis decided it was time to strike. They would control humans using something they couldn't resist.

The food.

Haadis figured that if they could control the flow of food to humans, they could effectively control human actions. Through research and observation though, the monsters learned that humans aren't very collaborative while under duress. Cutting off their food supply would likely not only create a state of unrest but could also be a very unwieldy process, logistically. Haadis didn't want unwieldy. She didn't want duress. She wanted humans never to see it coming. She remembered The Plight of Iresine. She remembered it often, but this time she focused on what she saw before the killings began: all of the gluttony and hedonism with regard to the tasty treats at the fair. That is how they would do it. The monsters would create delicious food for humans. They would do whatever was necessary to get them to purchase and eat it, in large volumes. Once the humans were addicted, and the business was successful enough, the monsters could do anything.

They could poison the humans. They could bleed them dry financially. As much as humans loved food, the monsters might be able to start a war! Either way, it was from this germ that the Methuselah of strategic plots, The Beach Apple, began to grow. The monsters were in for more and more years of small, stealthy victories. But it would be worth it. It would all be worth it.

This plan had launched itself over time into a full-fledged, multibillion dollar company. The Beach Apple had an upper hand in the market, because aside from shareholder value, operating and business expenses, all of the money the corporation made was pumped back into the business. More food, more advertising, more restaurants. Healthier food, faster, at lower prices. Monsters had never needed human currency, and aside from running the business, they still had no need for it. Not one monster grew corrupted; they weren't like humans. Worldly power and influence of this sort meant nothing to them. No monsters had or desired salaries; only the day-to-day human workers were paid. The puppeteers of the corporation were rarely visibly seen. Most of the important meetings were virtual conferences, or in dark, casual meeting rooms with long tables, which they had convinced the American leads was the order of business abroad. The monsters never did fully get the hang of the human-costumes. Their anatomies were so different that nothing ever felt both comfortable and convincing. So they used them sparingly. The backstory was that The Beach Apple, which had begun as a small private franchise in Turkey, had migrated to the United States with the hope of prospering by way of its superior business model and unique positioning in the market. *The executives have no intention of transporting the company, but would rather manage the U.S. affairs from afar, considering the American Beach Apple business as somewhat sovereign,* was a constant refrain. It was perfect. Even though the corporate officers in America had the agency to make changes within the company, the business was so profitable that there was no immediately recognizable need. It was a golden goose among business people. The monsters also chose the most greedy, self-serving humans for the lead positions. This would ensure that those employees never tried to better anyone's situation but their own and would likely remain disinterested in effecting change for the greater good within the corporation.

Which brings us back to present times. The monsters were observing the last of many focus groups that had confirmed their favorability in the market with consumers. Monsters had humans eating out of the palms of their hands, figuratively and literally. A group vote had decided the fate of the humans; they would be poisoned. They had experimented with the poison in food before in small doses and believed it would have the desired effect when applied properly. The systemic poisoning would kill many humans very quickly, based on consumption statistics. By the time humans realized what was going on, the monsters would be in a good position to strike against government buildings, universities, and military bases. The monsters had spent decades not only repopulating, but familiarizing themselves with human warfare, weapons, and defense. The Beach Apple was frequently a caterer to or featured at schools, Army bases, police stations, sporting events, and more. Haadis, Vedon, and the others were confident that if the timing was right, their coup d'état would meet with no significant resistance. They would soon be in control, after which they planned to eradicate the remainder of the humans, and begin the long process of rehabilitating the Earth. It was almost time.

***

"I just don't understand how you all can turn a blind eye to the fact that people have *died* eating this food. There have been multiple lawsuits with claims that all types of crazy stuff were found in the soups, salads, and whatever else. There was also that huge poison thing last year. The scientists couldn't even identify the chemical that was in the meat; they had never seen it before. So sure, there's a mistrial in the common law suit, but people died eating this food. And you can look me in my eyes and tell me that because people don't know this, they're better off? I'm sorry. I have more faith in people than that. I'd like to believe that knowing and understanding these types of things can make a difference."

The participants had to credit Lyn, who had remained as annoying throughout the focus group as in the beginning.

"Dal, how would Indira feel if something happened to the kids from eating this food every day? Especially now that you *know* it's not what you think it is. Could you sleep at night? And Sade. You and your friends want to grab food, and they want to eat this Beach Apple bullshit. You going with them just because? What kind of friends are these that won't take the three seconds it takes to care enough about a friend to choose something that's good for everyone?"

"You make sense, Lyn...It's just tha--"

"And you..." Lynn interrupted, glaring at Cecily. "You're really not any different than me. You're just on the other team. But you're the worst kind. You know better and choose not to do better, just so everyone can get on, most of us with lives we don't even like all that much. Not everybody can see what's going on, but you can. And instead of helping others to make better decisions, you'd rather just go through the motions, because you're too fucking cool to really care about anything."

"Hey now!" snapped Marjorie.

"Sorry," said Lyn. "I'm just saying. I hope you've thought about how you'd feel if all your friends were as faux apathetic as you, and you were in need. When you're lost in the dark, without a leg to stand on, and someone says, 'Shit happens,' I wonder if you'll regret every time you could have been a raft on the river for someone, but chose to let them drown."

Cecily was quiet for a moment. She glanced at Lyn over the top of her glasses and gave the slightest, most dismissive eye roll she could muster.

"Let's take a look at our final advertising material, and then I have a closing question based on everything we've seen today."

Marjorie passed a small stack of cards to Dal, who passed it around to the rest of the participants. They were coupons, the kind that find their way into your mailbox when you move to a new neighborhood. They were completely blue, with a small square photo of a family laughing while eating at a dinner table in the middle. White script below the photo read:

Welcome to the neighborhood. Why don't you join us for dinner?

Below the message would be the address to the Beach Apple closest to where the new folks had moved. It was a simple piece, but the group pondered it for a while without speaking. Sade was first.

"The togetherness. The warmth. The gesture of inviting you to dinner once you've moved into an unfamiliar place. This is...this is really brilliant." She spoke sadly, her voice sounding as if she could cry at any moment. She put the card down and put her face in her hands.

"I agree, this is great," said Dal.

"Cute," said Cecily.

Lyn's eyes scanned the room until settling back on the card. Lyn looked at Marjorie, and then pushed the card away, toward the center of the table, and shrugged.

"Very well then," said Marjorie. "I believe you all have received your compensation for your time today, which we appreciate. If you leave this room and go right, the exit of the building is downstairs to the left. The security guard will show you out down there. As promised though, I have a final question I'd like to ask you all, based on all of the materials we saw and discussion we engaged in today. What is your opinion of the Beach Apple? And if it's negative, what could the restaurant do to change your opinion?"

"It's great restaurant," said Dal. "It keeps my kids happy, which is more than I can ask for in this life."

"I think the whole corporation is a piece of shit. It's one thing to offer food that could potentially kill your customers. It's another to have the audacity to parade the menu around as if it's saving lives when in actuality it's destroying them. There's no replacement for integrity. And there's nothing they can do to change my mind."

It was Lyn.

"You're so unforgiving, Lyn. Some of us have never done anything wrong, I guess, huh? The restaurant is cute; like I said, I like their burrito bowls. I think they could probably do less in the way of cheesy advertising and speak more to the arts crowd, which is really the heart and soul of this city. So maybe localizing the ads more. But, I mean, I'm not a suit or anything. Just think it'd help 'em."

Cecily stared at Lyn until Lyn looked back.

"See? Helpful enough for you?" Cecily asked.

"Fuck off."

"Sure. Have fun living your life on the run. You talk about having faith in people. Ha! All this condemnation of 'liars' you've been doing today, and you're lying to yourself. You're too scared to trust anybody or anything because *everything* is a setup and *everybody* is out to get you, right? Would love to see what kind of meaningful relationships you form," Cecily said with a patronizing smile.

All eyes turned to Sade.

"Well...aw jeez. When I first came here, I was really on the fence about this place. And I think that there are definitely pros and cons to the way that the corporation presents itself, but that's the same with anything. They're different...but everybody loves them, which has to count for something. I know how it feels to be different and unloved. I know how hard it is. So the fact that they've mastered the craft is admirable. I don't know much about nutrition and fancy chemicals. But I know that if I had got that coupon card in the mail, I'd feel like I had a friend. It seems like they care, and like Cecily said, it's hard to do everything right. But they're trying, it seems. And that has to count for something, right? I would definitely say I'm more of a supporter of The Beach Apple now than I was when I first came here. I think they're really trying to do a good thing."

Lyn's eyes pleaded with Sade. She sensed it.

"I know, Lyn; I know what you're thinking. But I think you're thinking a little too hard. You have to enjoy the times when everything is just fine and cross the burning bridges when you get to 'em, you know?"

Lyn turned away from the table toward the viewing glass. For a brief second, it appeared as if something was moving behind it. Lyn knew that there were people observing the group, but she had forgotten during the course of the night and was startled by the motion. Lyn's gaze lingered for a few more seconds until the glass looked completely still and dark once more.

***

The group exited the research building and went their separate ways: Dal back to his family, Cecily back to her friends, Lyn back to the hovel, and Sade back into obscurity. She had actually enjoyed the focus group. It was the first time in a long while that she had spoken with others who seemed to care about her opinion. Each one exited through the turnstile at the bottom of the stairs and went left through the revolving doors. Sade and Dal disappeared quickly into the warm night air. Cecily lingered, waiting for a cab. Just as one arrived and she opened its door, Lyn called out to her.

"What?"

"All that stuff you said up there," Lyn said solemnly.

"Yeah?"

"I was thinking about it...and I realized something."

Cecily puffed her cigarette in silence.

"I realized that it's going to take a really profound pain to shake you out of your listlessness. Something terrible is going to happen to you or someone you love. You'll probably wake up after that. For your sake, I just hope it doesn't happen too much later from now. You're already a mess."

Cecily flicked her half-finished cigarette at Lyn's feet.

"You're a monster."

As the cab sped away toward the city, Lyn bent down, picked up the cigarette, and took a puff. Stress. After having quit for the third time that morning, Lyn would have to start over yet again. Lyn turned and threw down the cigarette, much too late in noticing someone approaching from the very same direction in which the butt was tossed. It hit the foot of the pedestrian, and this person, inches from Lyn at this point growled, "Watch it!!!" in a hoarse, throaty tone. As he pushed past Lyn, Lyn noticed what looked like purple skin protruding from under the flesh-colored skin on his collarbone. Shocked momentarily, Lyn shook herself out of it eventually, picked up the cigarette butt, and took one last puff. Upstairs, the last illuminated room in the research building went dark. The monsters would reconvene and talk about the findings from the latest focus group tomorrow. Haadis would proudly announce that The Beach Apple had achieved enough longstanding favorability in the market for the monsters to enact the final phase of their plan. They had waited some time for this. Their ancestors would be proud.

After two cabs bypassed Lyn, it started raining. Lyn turned and looked down the street toward the residential part of the city. It was only a couple blocks away from home, might as well walk. The thought of the motion behind the dark glass kept swirling in Lyn's mind. Was it a face that had pulled back from the glass so rapidly? Lyn imagined a dragon-like creature, with rough, scaly skin and jagged teeth, licking its chops as it salivated over the humans from behind the glass. The thought made Lyn chuckle at first and then fearful. Either way, the rain was starting to come down harder. If only one could walk between the drops. About halfway home, Lyn's stomach rumbled furiously. *What am I going to eat?* It was a fair question. One restaurant came immediately to mind.

Afterword

This art is dear to me, not simply because it's my first book, but because of what it means, more specifically, the multiplicity of its meanings. The epigraph of the work exposes us to one of the major flaws in human nature: our inclination to dream. The capacity to internalize sights, sounds, conversations, and experiences in our lives or others' lives, and to use those to develop a projection of what life could one day become, however romanticized, is both a very powerful and dangerous ability. The very same ability that hinders us enables us.

Thus, as we see with a majority of the protagonists in these tales, life's strategy never departs from positive visualization, but instead shifts to positive *realistic* visualization based on the harsh and sometimes painful experiential learning that living a full life necessitates. The learning to which youth and naiveté condemn us.

In planning to explain that my book looks to explore that aspect of human nature and draw inferences about the greater human condition while also integrating civil rights folklore, commentary on the black American condition, young adulthood, magical realism, and fairy tales, I expected backlash. I expected confusion. But I truly believe that the art is an embodiment of myself and every animate and inanimate thing on this Earth, as we hold the truth to be self-evident that everything we know, everything that is real to us, is multifaceted. It is my view that every topic has history. Every story is a journey or part of one. If we imagine these topics with historical prevalence as metaphorical roads, we know that one can only travel so long on any single road without it intersecting with another. It is an aspect of the inevitable beauty of art and life; things will collide. I consider myself only to have taken roads that readers normally choose not to travel simultaneously, and intersected them in the manner that makes the most sense to me, in an effort to show how beautiful it can be when all the individual parts of what makes you, "*You*," come together.

My hope is that this provides a read that is fresh and engaging and thought-provoking, more than anything else. Some readers have commented on the brevity of my stories, to which I say no story has a finite beginning or end. We are all threads woven together in life's fabric, constantly creating new stories in our relations with others, branches on a great tree of human experience. My stories are short because the art is less about what I have to say, and more about what the reader is capable of imagining. I want to speak to the inner dreamer of each reader; I want to create an artist from every audience member. If a story leaves you searching for pages to turn where none remains, you will turn to your imagination. You will create. I consider this a success for myself and for you as well.

But of dreams, this art is borne of them, both figuratively and literally. I wrote "The Southern District," barely awake in the pre-dawn hours in 2010, scrambling quietly in my room, scribbling down every detail I could remember before it fled my mind. My giddy excitement was barely containable as I weighed the risk of waking my roommate.

Now, my completed manuscript barely seems the work of the boy who once dreamed of himself in a lion suit, sporting a top hat. But I know it is. I am living his dream, the dream of telling the stories that our people want and need to hear, but have neither the words nor the voice to narrate. This art is borne from the dream that a kid from Atlanta with no business partners and no experience could successfully deliver a quality literary experience to the world because he believed he could. This art is borne out of the belief transformed into reality that anything is possible, with the right approach, the right timing, and God's favor. It is my hope that if none of the stories touch you, and none of the illustrations stir you, that the story behind the story — the birth of the art itself — can inspire you to do great things. For each of us is extraordinary, but similar to many of my favorite fairy tales, that is only as true as we believe it to be.

Yours,

hh

November 2, 2015

About the Author

H.D. Hunter is an Atlanta native and an alumnus of both Emory University and Wake Forest University School of Business. His passions include activism, travel, mentorship, and cinema. He is a member of Omega Psi Phi Fraternity, Inc. *A Magic Door and A Lost Kingdom of Peace* is his first book.

About the Illustrator

Donahue Johnson is a twenty-three year-old illustrator/ graphic designer living in the Greater Atlanta area. He is an alumnus of the unsinkable Albany State University and a member of Omega Psi Phi Fraternity, Inc.